WILD

LOVE

WILDING PACK WOLVES 2

ALISA WOODS

January 2016 Edition
Sworn Secrets Publishing

Cover Design by Steven Novak

ISBN-13: 978-1532729492
ISBN-10: 1532729499

Wild Love (Wilding Pack Wolves 2)

SWIPE RIGHT FOR WILDLOVE!
**She programs a dating app for shifters.
He's an ex-Army shifter with a dark secret.
The human and shifter worlds are about to collide…**

Noah Wilding's family is being targeted by an anti-shifter hate group—so he took a medical leave from the Army to return home and help out. At least, that's the story he's told everyone… and he hopes his dark secret will stay buried in Afghanistan.

Emily Jones is the lead programmer for WildLove, the new app that hooks up shifters and humans for a night of hot sex and no commitments. Only she hasn't had a date herself in years… ever since that dark day when her family didn't protect her when she needed them most. She figures one magical night with a hot wolf will help her finally move on with her life.

When Noah swipes right for Emily, she thinks her dream one-night-stand is about to come true. But with a hate group planting car bombs during WildLove hookups, Noah and Emily are on the front lines of love. They have to hunt down a killer before he strikes again… and before they do more than heat up the sheets. Because humans and shifters might get "Wild for a Night"… but they're not supposed to fall in love.

CHAPTER 1

Noah Wilding hiked up the stairs to the second floor of the motel. He couldn't decide if he wanted this time to be like the last three hookups—a couple hours of raging hot sex with a human female until both of them were worn out from the sheer intensity and repeated orgasms—or if he wanted to finally flush out the bad guy so his pack could catch the bastard.

Tough choice.

"How about you leave the mic on this time, Noah?"

The voice coming over his earbud was scratched with a bit of static, but he easily recognized Jimmy, who could give him a run for *Horniest Unmated Wolf* in the River pack. The kid was barely eighteen to Noah's twenty-one and would've traded places with Noah in a heartbeat.

"Or maybe you could just get the job done a little faster?" That was Jace River, his sister's mate and one of the three River brothers who ran Riverwise, the security firm that Noah, Jimmy, and the rest of the pack worked for. "I mean, really? Two hours. What takes you so long?"

Laughter came over the earbud from the rest of the assholes in the pack van.

"Come on, man, leave the mic on." Jimmy again, pleading. "I want to learn from the Master."

"You guys are a bunch of perverts," he whispered into his mic, which was sewn into his collar. He tried not to be obvious about talking into his clothes, not that there was anyone lingering around the motel balcony at ten o'clock at night for this app-mediated booty call. "If you losers weren't all so ugly, maybe you could be on the front lines like me." He smirked at the roar of protests that flooded his earbud.

Noah paused at the door—number twenty-three—

trying to get in the right frame of mind and forget the assholes who were listening in.

He pictured the face he had seen on the WildLove app—pretty, young like him, sparkling blue eyes—just the kind of soft, innocent-looking face that would lure in a hot-blooded shifter. This new dating app run by the Seattle Shifters Dating Agency had gotten wildly popular once a hate group decided to start targeting shifters. That had cleared out the downtown shifter bars—it just wasn't safe to gather in groups these days—which left a lot of shifters very horny with not a lot to do about it. The app was genius for hooking up shifters with willing humans, which was apparently the new rage among Seattle's hipsters… until someone started planting car bombs while the couple was tangled in the sheets.

Two shifters had been hit in the last two months—both survived, but that only proved how damn hard it was to kill them. Riverwise had teamed up with the dating agency to go undercover and hunt down whoever was doing this before they succeeding in killing someone… not to mention put the dating agency out of business.

Which was why he was here.

"Okay, perverts," Noah whispered into his mic. "I'm going in. Mic is switching off, but let me know if you see anything. And keep your chatter to a minimum. It's hard to get it up with you guys in my ear."

He tapped the mic off and chuckled at the predictable swearing and good-natured name-calling that followed, but they quickly settled down. He knocked on the door—three quick raps—and tried to get his game face on.

When the door opened, the girl inside looked just like her picture—only instead of sweet-and-innocent, she was smokin' hot. The nerdy T-shirt and jeans from her WildLove profile had been replaced by a silky dress that clung to her luscious curves in all the right places. But as hot as she was, standing there holding the door open, she seemed as skittish as a startled kitten.

"Um…hi," he said, working to keep the drool in his mouth. "I'm Noah Wilding." He sincerely hoped there would be no bad guys tonight. If this human girl wanted a taste of wolf, he definitely wanted to help out with that.

She blinked, rapidly, and her mouth opened, but nothing came out. She was checking him out, but in a nervous kind of way, as if she was fighting it—flicking her eyes down to his chest and even lower, then jerking them back up again. And she was biting her lip like she was trying to chew it off.

When she didn't say anything, he frowned and added, "I'm, you know, from WildLove?" He glanced at the door number, even though he was sure this was the girl. But if she was too freaked out by the hookup, he wanted to give her a plausible excuse to bow out. "Is this the right room?"

"Oh yeah. I mean, *yes*. The right room. Definitely!" She squeezed her eyes tight for a second like she was trying to get a grip on herself.

He grinned. She was fucking *adorable*. Man, he hoped she would actually invite him in.

She finally opened her eyes again. "Please come in." She visibly swallowed and stepped back to give him room.

He slowly stepped inside, like any sudden movement might scare her off. The room was pretty standard for a low-rent motel room—cheesy art on the walls, really thin spread on the bed, worn patterns in the industrial carpet. He gave it a good checking out, just in case. The previous attempts had been car bombs, not traps lurking in the motel room itself, but that was still a possibility. He turned back to her and watched her close the door with shaky hands.

Why was she so nervous? The last three women had

definitely been… *experienced* in this sort of thing. The previously-vibrant shifter bar scene meant there were a lot of human females who had scored a little paranormal action before. But if he was being set up…

"You *are* Emily Richards, right?" That was the name on her profile… who knew what it was in real life. Almost no one used their real names on WildLove. He had used his because the freak who was head of the hate group—a guy who called himself the Wolf Hunter—had already outed all the Wilding pack members, including Noah. And that made him a tempting target.

The girl's back was glued to the door, hands flat against it. "Yes. My name is Emily." There was a kind of terror in her eyes, and her long blond hair didn't quite hide the shaking of her shoulders.

He waited for more, but it wasn't forthcoming. This girl was either freaked about setting him up and had an accomplice outside, or this was just her first time with a shifter. A few whispers floated across his earbud, but nothing to indicate anything was wrong in the pack van.

Noah narrowed his eyes. "We really don't have to do this, if you don't want to." He held his hands out, palms forward, like he was calming a wild rabbit.

That seemed to rise up some fire in her. She pushed

away from the door and took three determined strides toward him, stopping just inside his reach. *"No."* She sucked in a breath. "I want to do this."

She was obviously trying to be brave about this for some reason, but the twitchy look on her face was bringing out the protective side of his wolf. His inner beast was no ordinary wolf, but it was still *all alpha*... and that skittish look was just making him want her more. Like his wolf was dying to kiss away whatever was making her tremble.

"Okay." He swallowed, unsure how to proceed. Normally there was a little *banter* or *something* before the clothes started coming off. Although one of his hookups had barely said hello before she was tearing off his shirt. But this one... it felt like they should have gone out on a date, or three, before getting to this point, standing in a motel room together.

He held out his hand. She stared at it like it might bite her... then she slowly put her hand in his. It was warm and soft and delicate, with thin little fingers that looked like they hadn't done any manual labor in her entire life.

"What do you do for a living, Emily?" he asked, pulling her a little closer and capturing her pretty blue eyes with a gentle look. She was short, and he kind of loomed over her, but he hoped his touch and a little small talk would calm her. Besides, WildLove was pretty scant on personal details, given it was a site primarily designed for brief sexual encounters with no chance of commitment. He really didn't know anything about her.

"Um…" She swallowed again, peering up at him, but not moving away. "Librarian."

He smiled. "You're kidding me. A sexy librarian? How did I get so lucky?" He was close enough to put his arms around her now, but he was still just holding her hand. He had a sudden urge to pull her into a hug—a protective, reassuring one—but even that seem too *intimate*. Too fast. Instead, he tucked her hand against his chest.

"I'm not going to hurt you, Emily."

Her eyes grew a little wider. "I know," she whispered. "Shifters are extremely protective of their mates, and even women and children they don't know but need their help. In fact, it's been widely shown that they rarely attack anyone without provocation, much less someone weaker or more vulnerable than them, which is really pretty much any human. Their whole pack culture is wrapped up in family and caring and a tight magical bond of love." She stopped suddenly, the look of terror scuttling back to her face, like she hadn't meant to blurt all that out at once.

Noah just stared. She certainly talked like a librarian. But it was more than a little weird to have that kind of encyclopedic knowledge of shifters—and it was just the kind of research someone obsessed might do. Obsessed enough to kill.

"You seem to know a lot about shifters," he said carefully.

Her cheeks flushed. She dropped her gaze to the floor, then the bed, then the wall... anywhere but looking at him. "I just... I just think shifters are..." Her gaze finally came back to him, fixing on his chest. "Amazing," she breathed out. Then she slowly dragged her gaze up to meet his. Her lips parted, and she seemed to be laboring to breathe.

Noah knew women reacted to the alpha-ness inside him. His shifter body, the muscles that turned women on, the military bearing he carried from his time in the Army—all of it had an effect. He'd seen it in action too many times not to be aware of it. But this... this girl's wide-eyed breathlessness... maybe it wasn't just her first time with a shifter.

Maybe it was her first time *ever.*

That set his nerves on end. Partly because he hadn't been with a virgin since he was one himself, and that was years ago. Partly because that blue-eyed innocence was working some kind of magic on his cock. His head and body were in a war with one another, one wanting to dive right into tasting her while the other wanted to hold back. Plus, this could still be a setup. She wasn't a casual human looking for a casual fuck. Which pointed to obsession. Which might mean the hate group he was trying to trap.

The whole thing felt like rocky ground, but there was nothing to do but walk over it and test it out. "So that's why you're here—you want to know what it's like to be with one of us."

"Yes." She let out a breath that was maybe relief.

He pulled her even closer.

Her eyes dilated, and her breathing picked up. The scent of her arousal surged over the fresh-washed clean-skin smell, no perfume but the lovely scent of *her,* that was also drawing him in. That finally convinced him to shove aside his suspicions and go for his original purpose—which was to take the delicious human bait of whoever was attempting to murder shifters by planting bombs in their cars.

Noah ran a finger slowly across Emily's cheek. She closed her eyes with his touch and shuddered a little. He cupped her face with his hand and leaned in, close enough to kiss, but still not touching.

"You're new to this, right?" he whispered.

She blinked open her eyes and nodded, quickly.

He pulled back a little to look in her eyes. "I'm going to say this straight out because there's really not another way to ask."

"Okay," she breathed. It struck him that she actually *was* brave, in spite of the quaking. After all, she was alone in a room with a shifter. Compared to her, he was a dangerous thing. And that was without her even knowing the truth about his abilities or how fucked up he really was.

"You haven't done this before," he said softly.

"Right." Her eyes were wide.

He paused for a second, then added, "I mean, you haven't done this *having sex* thing before."

Her eyes went even more wide, then she dropped her gaze to the floor. "No, I have."

That wasn't the answer he expected. "So you're not a virgin?" At twenty-one or so, it wasn't like it was impossible. Or unheard of.

She looked up, but just barely, almost like she couldn't look him in the eye. "No." Then nothing more.

The awkward silence was shoved aside by laughter from the guys in the surveillance van. Of course, Emily couldn't hear it, but it still make him cringe.

Suddenly, her gaze was demanding. "Does that matter?"

He frowned. "No, I just wanted to make sure—"

She pulled back and wrapped her arms tight around her chest. "How do I know you're even a wolf?" she demanded.

The question knocked him back. None of the others had asked—they were more than happy to climb up on his cock without proof he was a shifter, much less which kind. It wasn't like they were looking to settle down and have half-breed shifter pups. Humans and shifters got it on, but they didn't mate—at least, not often. And now, with the hate flames being fanned even more, the few intermarrying couples definitely kept that in the closet. He wasn't mate material anyway, for shifters or humans. Female shifters were in short supply, and they usually went for the strongest alpha they could find, not genetic freaks like him. Besides, his own family proved that mating could be a curse as much as a blessing.

Noah struggled for something to say. "I guess… I could *show* you I'm a wolf."

He fully expected that to drive her away completely.

Instead, her eyes lit up. "Really? You'd shift for me?"

He grimaced. This seemed… really unwise. Especially given the unusual nature of his wolf form these days. But her arousal scent was through the roof. He was definitely turning her on. And he needed to draw this thing out to give whoever might be planting a bomb time to do so.

"Sure," he said, against his better judgment. He nearly turned the mic back on but decided against it. After all, this girl wasn't capable of hurting him directly, even if she was setting him up. So, he held her gaze for a moment and then quickly shifted.

She gasped and both hands flew to her mouth, but she didn't back away. He knew what she saw—a white, shaggy wolf with oversized fangs and crystal-blue eyes. He kept his claws sheathed because she didn't need that nightmare in her head. This wasn't the wolf he was born with… it was the result of experiments the government had done on him, bringing out something that had been buried in his genetic code. *The family secret*. He hadn't shifted for anyone since he'd taken that medical leave and gotten the hell out of Afghanistan. His cover story was that he came home to protect his family, the sprawling Wilding pack… but the truth was much more complicated.

Emily dropped her hands from her mouth and edged toward him, hand extended. "Can I touch you?" she asked, voice full of breathy excitement.

He dipped his head.

She ran one hand through the fur at the top of his head, then brought the other up as well. He leaned into her a little—her gentle massage actually felt pretty good.

"A white wolf," she breathed. "So rare as to be almost legend. I can't believe… of all the luck… wolves like you are said to be almost magical. Not the normal shifter magic, but more so. Like a cross with witches, perhaps in ancient times, before the paranormal creatures split up into different—"

He cut her off by nuzzling her arm, gently but enough to stop the history report. It was starting to freak him out.

She pulled back and looked directly into his eyes, her face only inches away. "You are *so* beautiful."

Okay, that was enough. He shifted quickly, capturing her in his arms before she could back away. It took less than a fraction of a second and wrenched a gasp out of her, but by the time it was done, he was holding her in his arms and pulling her against his naked body.

"We usually prefer the term *handsome,*" he said with a smirk.

Then he kissed her.

Damn, she was soft—the dress, her silky blonde hair spilling over his hands, her lips melting under his. It took her a second, but then she was all over him in return—small hands clawing at his shoulders, tongue eager in his mouth, her skirt hiking up as she hitched one of those luscious legs over his bare hip, bringing her body even closer. He slipped a hand inside the soft silk of her dress and cupped her breast, moaning as he found her nipple already hard for him. His cock sat up and pressed into the infinite softness that was her body—and he was instantly aching to bury it in her for real.

He pulled back from the kiss to lower his mouth to her neck.

She moaned and tipped her head back.

"You have too many clothes on," he whispered between wet nips at her skin.

"Yes," she breathed.

He backed her toward the bed, slowly. They'd gone zero-to-sixty in less than five seconds—there was something about her obsession with shifters that was sending his wolf into overdrive—and he seriously hoped she was telling the truth about not being a virgin. Because he was suddenly dying to take her hard, slamming the flimsy motel bed against the wall and hearing her scream out his name.

If she liked wolves before, he aimed to make her a permanent fan.

He had her nearly to the bed—and her dress inched up past her waist—when voices suddenly exploded in his ear.

"Ten o'clock!"

"I see him!"

"What the fuck—"

"Jimmy, stay here. Murphy, Simpson, take the far flank. Ashton, you're with me. Go, go, go!"

Noah yanked back from kissing Emily. Something was going *down* outside, and he was standing in the motel room, naked with a hard-on. *Shit.*

He abruptly left Emily teetering at the bedside and raced back to where his clothes lay in a heap on the musty carpet. As he hurriedly pulled them on, she was sputtering out something while wrapping her arms tightly around herself again.

"I have to go," he said, roughly, yanking his shirt over his head. The shouts were growing louder and more frantic in his ear.

"I... did I... do something wrong?" She was shaking.

Fuck. He didn't know if she was involved in this, whatever it was, or if she was just an innocent bystander, but he didn't have time to explain.

"I just have to go." He shoved on his shoes and raced to the door. Right before he reached it, he heard a series of pops that had to be gunfire. *Shit!* He flung it open, lurched outside, and remembered to turn on his mic. "What the hell's going on?" he shouted over the growls and grunts coming through his earbud. He raced to the end of the balcony where he could to get a good look at his car and the van parked below. His pack had swarmed over a guy, taking him down hard against the pavement. One of them had shifted, but he was lying prone on the ground while the others held the perp down.

Noah pounded down the stairs and hauled ass toward the downed wolf.

No, no, no... its relatively slender body, short-cut brown fur... it had to be Jimmy.

Noah reached Jace's side, where he was bent over Jimmy. Jace had been a medic in the Army, and he was already probing Jimmy's wound, which was somewhere on his head—it was covered in blood. Noah couldn't tell how bad it was, but he'd seen plenty of head wounds overseas, and they were bad news. Jimmy's eyes were closed, his face slack.

"Jace?" Noah held back, chest tight, not wanting to get in Jace's way.

His hands were all over Jimmy's head, feeling through the mess of fur and blood. "I think he's just knocked out," he said quickly. "Bullet only grazed him. But I need to get him in the van and stitch him up fast. Head wounds bleed like crazy."

Relief trickled through Noah. Jace wouldn't give that kind of hope if it weren't real. Noah and three others quickly lifted Jimmy and carried him back to the van. The rest stayed behind to cuff the asshole who shot him. Noah wanted to tear the man apart, but they needed him alive to figure out if he was acting alone. As they were climbing in the van, a movement caught Noah's eye—the girl, Emily, was staring at them from atop the balcony. He thought her expression was filled with horror, but he couldn't be sure from this distance. Then she quickly turned and fled.

He let her go. If she were involved, they could track

her down. If not, there was no reason for her to become part of this. He climbed into the van with the rest of his pack, hoping like crazy Jace could keep Jimmy alive.

CHAPTER 2

All Emily had wanted was *one night.*

One night with a shifter would have changed everything for her. She would have finally been able to put her past behind her and live her life again. She had tried with other men, but she could never get through a first date without having a panic attack. She knew, she just *knew,* it would be different with a wolf. Shifters were no ordinary men—they were all about pack and family and love—and she was certain she would be *safe* with one of them.

Only it had all gone wrong. And a shifter had been *shot*.

Emily dropped her head into her hands, gripping her hair and shaking her head. She'd been sitting at her desk and staring at her screen for an hour, trying to figure out how last night had gone from the most exciting night of her life to the most horrifying in an instant. It had also been the most electrifying and the most embarrassing… it was like all the things her life had never been, for better and worse, all wrapped up in a single, intense night at a dingy motel. Not even a whole night, as she had planned… just a few heart-stopping minutes.

Part of her was screaming that *this* was exactly why she didn't date. Why she only went out to movies with her friend, Sophie, never walked anywhere alone, and spent most of her nights at home with a good book and her cat, Peabody. It was a *boring* life, but it was a *safe* life. Another part of her was certain she had lived more in that brief period of time with Noah Wilding than in all the rest of her so-called "life" combined.

She raised her head and stared at the WildLove program on her screen. She should've known that putting herself in the database would've unraveled everything like crazy. It was the only thing she'd ever done that was even *slightly* against the rules. She was WildLove's lead programmer, for heaven's sake. It was her *job* to make sure it ran 24/7 without a hiccup, not to use it to score a date. She had just spent *so long* watching all the hookups happen, day after day—all those women who were *not her*, meeting insanely hot, super protective, *safe* shifter men. Was it so wrong that she wanted a small bit of that life for herself? She knew everything there was to know about shifters, and she was certain even one night would have changed everything.

She sighed, pushed away from her desk, and went in search of coffee. It only took a minute to brew her favorite chai latte in the breakroom Keurig, then she was back at her desk, a steaming cup by her keyboard, and still at a loss as to what had happened. The only thing to do was to erase last night from her memory… and from the WildLove database.

Her fingers flew over the keyboard while her coffee cooled.

She'd spent the last year hoping she might stumble upon a shifter the old-fashioned way, in a coffee shop or on her bus ride into work, even though she knew the odds of that were long. Shifters kept to the shadows for a reason—it was dangerous for them out on the streets, where the stupid humans of the city didn't understand how amazing they were. But she wasn't the kind of girl who could go to a shifter bar and meet someone there— she wouldn't make it two feet inside the door. That left her with coming into work every day and watching other people live her dream life. Putting herself in the WildLove database seemed like the perfect fix... but it wasn't until she saw Noah Wilding's profile pop up that she had actually gone through with it.

You're not a stalker, she told herself, although she was sure it would look that way to anyone peering in on her all-too-boring life. She followed all the news about *any* shifters—Noah and the Wilding pack had just been in the news *a lot*, so she knew all about him. The fact that he was outed by the hate group. The fact that he had served in Afghanistan. The horrible fact that his father was the disgraced Colonel Wilding, the man in charge of those terrible experiments that had been performed on shifters and exposed by Grace Krepky, the new openly-shifter candidate for the House of Representatives. It was about time shifters had a representative in the government! Emily knew that for sure.

But it was the heartbreaking story about Noah being

released from the experiments performed by his own father, going back overseas to serve his country in Afghanistan, only to come home again because his pack was being threatened that had captured her imagination. It was tragic and horrible and everything that made shifters and their packs brave and amazing. The magical bond they had tied them together stronger even than blood—and that was part of what she loved about them. Much more so than some of the humans she had encountered in her life, especially her supposed "family" who never protected her.

Not like she needed. Not when she needed it.

She pushed away those thoughts and brought up Noah's profile. He was insanely hot, just like all the shifter men—dreamy brown eyes, broad shoulders with all those shifter muscles. It was no random swipe that had brought up "Emily Richards" on his WildLove app. It had been easy to force the algorithms to make her profile come up while he was online, as well as keep the other excessively gorgeous female choices from showing, but there was no way she could make him actually swipe right for her. In fact, she had been certain he wouldn't. After all, she couldn't even bring herself to do one of those super-sexy poses the women on WildLove all seemed to have—makeup that oozed sex appeal and clothes they were practically spilling out of. Emily figured she had no chance against *that*. She was doing good to quickly paste in a picture from the company picnic last summer and upload before she lost her nerve.

But then he *did* swipe right for her. And suddenly her life was on fire with potential.

Right away, Noah had messaged her, asking for her number on the secure chat line. After several small heart attacks, she had worked up the courage to reply. WildLove was a hookup app, but sometimes people set up coffee dates first, maybe in public settings if they were worried. But most human females were on the app precisely because they want a *wild time*, not a boyfriend. And the shifters were also there for only one thing… and it wasn't to look for a mate. Most WildLovers went straight for a time and a place for the hookup. Noah was really sweet and funny in chat, but he quickly got down to business, and they had agreed to meet at that sleazy motel… and then the whole thing had turned into a disaster.

Even worse—if her boss found out, Emily would be fired in two seconds flat.

With her tech skills, she could make it all disappear—

there would be no evidence of any hookup between "Emily Richards" and Noah Wilding. But then she realized, she couldn't, not with how things went down. Her boss was sure to find out a shifter had been shot at a WildLove hookup. How could she not? Emily had fled the scene, but the police must've been called in and reports must've been made. She prayed the shifter who had been shot—the one Noah had run out to help—had survived. And there was something really strange about there being other shifters there that night, and even more weird that somehow they'd been attacked. But she figured the motel must have all kinds of shady dealings going on. She and Noah certainly weren't the WildLovers hooking up last night.

But somewhere along the line, this shooting would get back to the agency and Emily's boss. Someone would search the records, and it would be obvious that *she* was Emily Jones, the short girl with the long blonde hair and the serious character flaw of going after shifters who were totally out of her league. Erasing it would only make her look guilty of things she wasn't guilty of… namely being involved in the shooting.

So, she couldn't erase last night… but she could try to scour any evidence that pointed to her. She brought up the WildLove database, snagged a picture off another Internet dating site, and swapped it for her profile. The woman looked somewhat like her—same long blonde hair, same age and roundish kind of face—and the fake name could stay. She'd already been careful not to put any identifying features in her profile and used an untraceable account for the secure chat room.

If anyone went on WildLove now, there would be nothing to tie her, Emily *Jones,* to the Emily *Richards* that Noah had met the night before. And she doubted he would remember her well enough to realize the picture of the girl was any different from the person he actually met. The only thing that could trip her up was if someone went through the backups and change records and found the substitution. Or if someone had screencapped her profile before the change. Noah was her first and only WildLove hookup—she hadn't even answered any of the other messages—so she was probably safe with that. Her fingers flew over the keyboard again, accessing all the backups and changing them so there was no trace of what she had done.

Emily picked up her mug—it was the one with *Coffee is My Boyfriend* emblazoned on it—and breathed in the creamy spice smell of her latte. Then she closed her eyes and breathed out all the anxieties that had wrapped her in a tight ball since she'd stumbled home from the disaster non-hookup last night. Over the sacred fumes of her coffee, she vowed never to be so *stupid* again. She'd had her one chance with a shifter, and that was that. She would go back to her normal, sane, boring life, and count herself lucky for it.

"Are you going to breathe that or drink it?" a raspy voice said from the door.

It made her jump, pop open her eyes, and spill coffee on her keyboard. Groaning, Emily quickly set the mug down and snatched up her wireless keyboard to shake the liquid off before it could sink in. Then she glared at the source of the voice—her boss, Marjorie Simmons, aging hipster and CEO of the Seattle Shifters Dating Agency.

"Geez, Marjorie," Emily said, "give me a heart attack, why don't you?"

"Girlfriend, you *need* a little heart action." She smirked that little knowing smile she often had. Marjorie was a sex-obsessed old lady—okay probably only about sixty—one of those artsy Seattle types who knew all the best places to get coffee, hung out at all the poetry readings and art jams in the city, and knew absolutely everyone who was anyone. She was far more hip than Emily, and way too Zen to be the boss of a multi-million dollar company.

Plus Marjorie had more excitement in a single month than Emily had in her entire life—and definitely more sex. She was always off with a new boyfriend. The whole idea of WildLove had been her brainchild one day over coffee. Emily was working her way through college as a barista when Marjorie shared her sketched-out-on-a-napkin plan she had just come up with. Emily had simply said it wouldn't be that hard, technology-wise, to implement and boom! Marjorie hired her on the spot as lead developer for the app.

Emily had almost graduated from the University of Washington with her computer science degree, and there were already a lot of dating apps out there, so it wasn't too much of a stretch. Putting in security protocols for the chatroom had been a little tricky, but Marjorie agreed that protecting shifter anonymity was paramount. And funding had been no limit. Marjorie effortlessly brought in a ton of investment money from "a few of her friends." As soon as it was live, WildLove just took off. The rise of the shifter-haters had made it even more popular, as shifters stopping going to the bars and started looking for safer ways to hookup. Plus shifters were out in the open now, buzzing up all the tabloids.

WildLove was just the right idea at the right time.

Stuff like that happened to Marjorie. And ever since Emily started working at Seattle Shifters, Marjorie had been trying to rub some of that magic pixie dust off on her—specifically, trying to hook Emily up with guys. Of course, dipping into WildLove as her personal dating playground was strictly off-limits, as it was for all employees. It was right there in the employee handbook. Emily had read it.

"My heart is just fine the way it is," she lied a gigantic, monster-sized lie of ridiculousness. She hoped it didn't show on her face.

"Sure it is, kid," her boss said, her face wrinkling up with pity, although not too unkindly. "You've got a heart the size of Montana—don't think I don't know it, just because you keep it all wrapped up tight in those little sweaters you wear in the middle of July."

Emily pulled her sweater tighter across her chest. "It gets chilly in here with the air conditioning."

Marjorie just nodded. "Listen, sweetie, I've got some bad news. I've been keeping this from you because I know what a soft heart you have for our shifters. And I sure like that part about you, but I need your help with something now, so I need to tell you."

Emily swiveled her chair to face Marjorie a little better. "Sure, Marge, you know I'll do anything for you. And Seattle Shifters. You guys are my life."

Marjorie gave her a sad look. "Damn shame that is, too. But never mind all that." She sucked in a breath and let it out slow. "I'm afraid that a couple of our hookups have gone, well, very badly. You know about the hate groups in the news, right?"

Emily nodded, and her heart started jumping around like an electrocuted rabbit. Oh God, did Marjorie *know?* Already?

Marjorie continued, "There was a shifter shot last night. He wasn't one of our customers, but the shooting *was* associated with a WildLove hookup."

Oh God, here it comes. "That's horrible," Emily squeaked.

Marjorie scowled. "Damn right it is! These bastards… I don't know where they get off targeting shifters when they should just look in the mirror and see where all the assholes in the world are. Motherfuckers!"

Emily managed not to wince. She'd gotten used to Marjorie's colorful language over the last year. "Is the shifter all right?"

Marjorie's anger quickly morphed into a smile. "Yes, sweetie, he is. You know how tough those sexy boys are."

Emily nodded, relieved.

"Anyway," her boss said, "this isn't the first time."

"It's not?" Emily's mind spun up fast. Wait… there were *more* attacks connected to WildLove? "Why haven't I heard anything about this on the news?" Now that she thought about it, she'd been so panicked about being caught, she hadn't even thought to watch the news last night.

"Well, as you probably know," her boss said, "I have a few friends in the shifter community. We've been working together to make sure this thing stays quiet. Partly because we don't want people to panic, and partly because we've been trying to find out who's using WildLove to stalk shifters. I've been working with the River brothers—you've heard of them, right? They run that security firm, Riverwise."

"Of course, I know all about them. They were in the news. The oldest brother, Jared, is married to our new House of Representatives candidate—"

Marjorie held up a hand to stop her. "Of course, sweetie, I should've known you'd be all over this."

Emily buttoned her lips together, determined not to

run off at the mouth again and accidentally spill things.

"The point is," Marjorie said solemnly, "last night, Riverwise caught one of the stalkers. Maybe *the* stalker. I'm hoping there's only one."

"Wait…" Emily's brain was just catching up. Noah Wilding had been working for Riverwise ever since he returned stateside. "So, last night, when the shifter was shot, Riverwise was trying to lay a trap for him?"

"That's right. The shifter was one of the Riverwise wolves. And it looks like they caught their bad guy."

Emily shoulders dropped, partly with relief, and partly because it all had become clear. Noah didn't pick her because he was actually looking for a hookup—he was trying to catch the hate group creeps who were targeting shifters. It made complete sense, but it also twisted her heart into knots. She had hoped to at least hold onto the memory of last night, of Noah Wilding choosing her and kissing her because he was actually attracted to her, even if it was only physical… but it was all just a setup. A fluke that he had swiped her and not someone else.

"Well… that's really great," Emily forced out. "I mean, I'm glad they caught him." She tried to blink away her broken heart, then realized something didn't make sense. "But what do you need my help with?"

"The first time, it could have been a coincidence that it happened at a WildLove hookup. The second time was too suspicious… that's when I brought Riverwise in. Now that they have the guy in custody, well, there doesn't seem to be any link between him and the human females involved in the first two hookups. We were hoping to find a connection, but… it's not looking promising so far. I'm afraid there might be someone inside the agency helping him find targets."

"Inside the agency?" Emily was aghast. "How could anyone here—"

Marjorie cut her off again with a raised hand. "I knew you wouldn't ever believe someone could be capable of this, but I'd like you to keep an open mind and scour the records. See if you can find some kind of connection between this hater and WildLove. Or some kind of security breach from the outside. Not everyone in the world is a good guy, Emily."

"I know that." Emily scowled. She knew all too well how evil people could be. And if she found someone here in the company who had hurt shifters… she'd find a tech way to ruin their lives. On top of turning them over to the police. "And of course, I'll help. I'll do anything I can to bring these people to justice."

Marjorie smiled, her large amber earrings glinting as she moved. "That's my girl. Come on over to my office. I have someone I want you to meet."

Emily nodded and hurried out of her chair to follow after Marjorie's long-strided walk down the hall. She kept her head down, breathing through her teeth, anger boiling inside her. The agency had recently hired a ton of people—programmers, database managers, hardware specialists—all to ramp up WildLove to keep up with demand. There were more new faces than experienced people at the company these days—a lot more than the six they had started the company with a year ago. They did background checks, but it was possible someone from the hate group had managed to infiltrate them. Whoever this mole was, it would be her honor to find them and make them pay.

She was so wrapped up in the fury of her thoughts that it wasn't until she rounded the corner into Marjorie's office that she even wondered who her boss wanted her to meet. When she saw who it was, she froze in her tracks and legitimately thought she might die on the spot.

Noah Wilding.

Holy shit.

He looked up from his phone at her standing in the

doorway, and his eyes went wide for a split second. Then he whipped back to looking at his phone again. He tapped a few things in, ignoring her. Emily just stood there with her life flashing before her eyes—*Noah Wilding was in her boss's office.* It was all going to come apart in the next two seconds.

She was doomed.

Marjorie had crossed the office to lean against her desk, looking very pleased with herself. "Noah Wilding, I'd like you to meet my lead programmer, Emily Jones." She barely held back her grin.

Emily just stood there, inarticulate in the doorway.

Noah finally looked up from his phone, but all sign of recognition was gone from his face. He tucked his phone in his pocket and stepped forward to extend his hand. "Nice to meet you, Emily Jones."

She stared at his hand for an embarrassingly long half second, then jerked her hand up to take it. Her small hand disappeared inside the gentle grip of his large one. His touch was just as electric as it had been the night before while simultaneously being warm and reassuring.

"Mr. Wilding," she managed to get out.

He dropped her hand and turned to Marjorie.

Her boss addressed them both. "Emily, I'd like you to

work with Noah to use whatever information the Riverwise people have gathered on this guy. I'm putting a hold on any further hookups until we've found whoever is involved in these attacks. I'll make some excuse about servers being down, but that won't hold water for long. And I don't want to be out of business for too long, either." She pushed away from her desk, eyeing both Emily and Noah as if she couldn't be more pleased to be throwing them together... almost as if this was her own personal matchmaking!

But Emily still sighed in relief. It was obvious that Marjorie didn't know Emily had been there last night, and so far, Noah wasn't spilling her secret. "Of course," she said to Marjorie, then turned to Noah. "I'll do whatever I can to help."

"Thank you," Noah said, but his voice was cool. Measuring. "Maybe we could get started right away?"

"Um... yeah. Sure. Okay." *God,* she was babbling. She needed to get out of Marjorie's office *now.*

Her boss was overly delighted with this. "Yes! Absolutely. You two run along." She turned back to her desk and called over her shoulder. "Keep me posted! I want WildLove up and running again as soon as it's safe."

Noah followed her as she scurried out of Marjorie's

office. Emily kept her head down, avoiding looking back as Noah trailed right behind her.

Holy shit! What was she going to say to him? What *could* she say? She kept her mouth shut, heading fast toward her cubicle, but then Noah's warm hand landed on her elbow. She jerked to a stop and spun to face him.

His face was livid. She cringed under his anger, but words were frozen in her throat. They had stopped by the break room. He glanced around—it was early and the office was still pretty empty—then tugged her into the room and closed the door. She backed up against it, trying to get some distance from him and that anger-filled look on his face.

He leaned close, pinning her against the door with the stone-cold look in his eyes. "Tell me it's not you," he growled.

"Not me?" she squeaked.

His jaw worked. *"Do not* tell me you weren't there last night. Shifters have a very keen sense of smell, Emily *Jones,* and I'd know your scent anywhere."

"I… no… yes, that was me!" She was having a hard time breathing.

"Did you set me up?" His voice was ice cold. "Are you one of these nutjobs who's hunting shifters?"

"What?" Her mouth hung open in surprise. "No! I would never do anything like that! You... I..." Her hands were up between them, proclaiming her innocence and almost touching his chest, he was so close. "I think shifters are..." She swallowed and tried to calm her racing heart. "You have to believe me. I'm the last person on earth who would ever hurt a shifter." She pleaded him with her eyes to believe her.

He eased back a little, frowning. "Why did you run?"

"Because I *work* for WildLove!" she said, exasperated.

This seemed to sway him a little because he gave her more room. "So... what? You were just looking for a hookup?"

Her face flushed, but of course, that was exactly what she was doing. "I just wanted one night. That's all." Her throat was closing up with a turmoil of emotion, but some sign of it must have worked its way out into her voice because he frowned and eased back more. "To be honest," she said, "I never thought you'd actually swipe right for me."

He pulled back and gave her a quizzical look. "Why not?"

She gaped at him. "Why not? Look at me!" She gestured to her standard office attire—worn jeans, flat tennis shoes, no makeup whatsoever, a black coder t-shirt with a knit cardigan over it. She really did get cold in the air conditioning, but her outfit blasted out *loser who writes code* not *hot IT professional.*

He gave her a look like she was crazy, but then just shook his head. "So it was just a coincidence that you were my hookup when this hater was trying to plant a bomb on my car?"

"It *was* a coincidence, I swear. At least… I didn't know anything about it." She bit her lip. "I saw a wolf got shot. Marjorie said he was working for Riverwise, but that he's okay. Is that true?"

He gave her a pinched look. "Yeah, that was Jimmy. He's fine now."

She let out a sigh of relief. "Good. That's good to hear." She hesitated to say the thought running through her head, but she had to know… "Why didn't you say something to Marjorie about me?"

He gave her a small smile. "It seemed *odd* that the lead programmer on WildLove would be a lunatic trying to kill wolves." The smile turned into a smirk. "And I figured that hot kiss earned you a chance to explain."

Hot… *what?* Was Noah Wilding actually flirting with her?

She closed her gaping mouth. "I… um… thank you."

His frown returned. "But I do think *someone* in your agency is targeting shifters. Or has access to your database somehow."

She nodded in fast agreement. "If there is, trust me, I'm going to find them."

That banished the frown and brought back a smile. "Sounds like you're just the girl for that job, too."

His smile heated her up from the inside out. "Just don't tell Marjorie what I did, *please*. She'll fire me."

"Okay, programmer girl," he said with a full smirk. "But you have to make me a promise in return."

Her eyes went wide. "What's that?"

He held out his hand. "Give me your phone."

She frowned but hurried to fish it out of her pocket and hand it to him. He bent over it, tapping something in. What in the world was he doing? Then he handed it back to her and leaned in close again, putting one hand on the door behind her.

"Next time you want a random hookup, don't be random. Call me." Then he lightly kissed her on the cheek.

It felt like it was on fire. Or maybe that was her entire body.

She just stared at him.

He smirked. "Now let's go catch some bad guys."

CHAPTER 3

"Wait… your hookup works at WildLove? But you don't think she's the mole?" That was his sister, Piper, taking none of this bullshit story Noah was feeding her. Even though it was the truth. At least, *he* believed it.

"The lead programmer," he said. "But yes."

"She's a *programmer?*" his brother asked with that arrogant tone he always has. "As in, she knows all the tech back doors in the software that *she* designed? In what universe is it possible that she's *not* the mole?"

Daniel was looking at him like he was crazy, which wasn't unusual. They'd spent their entire childhoods with Daniel believing he was the only sane one among the three of them. Of course, it was really *their father*—Colonel Wilding—who was batshit crazy, but they hadn't known any better. They were just kids.

"In the universe where *this* lead programmer is a sweet girl named Emily Jones. A girl who would rather eat her own lips than try to hurt a wolf." Noah's voice was climbing up to a growl. He already felt protective of her—she seemed to bring that out of his beast, although he didn't understand why—and he didn't need Daniel revving him up more.

They were standing on the front porch of the River family safehouse, a huge estate tucked into the mountains of Washington outside Seattle. The inside was teeming with Wilding pack members from the five families. The Wildings were spread out all over, hardly what you would call a real pack, but they were still wolves… and gathering together when faced with danger was natural.

Piper narrowed her eyes. "Just how far did you go with this hookup?"

Noah tilted his head at her. "Like that's any of your business."

She raised both eyebrows and tossed a look to their brother, Daniel. "It's personal for him."

Noah's mouth fell open. "What—"

"That's it," said Daniel. "You're off this case. We'll put you on—"

"Oh hell no! I work for Riverwise, *brother*. You're not my boss." Anger was a red heat crawling up his neck. "And I am *not* off this case. I've spent half the morning working with Emily, looking for a connection between this Richard Bately asshole we caught and the prior bombing incidents." He flicked a hand toward the back of the safehouse, where they had the WildLove bomber bound up in one of the cottages. Interrogations hadn't come up with much more than his name and some crazy hate rhetoric spouting out of his mouth. All of Riverwise wanted a piece of the man, but torture wasn't on the table, not with Jaxson overseeing the operation. He was pretty straight-arrow, not unlike Daniel. But turning the suspect over to law enforcement wouldn't get them what they needed, either—shifters usually couldn't trust the police to do what needed doing, and they just treated shifters like second-class citizens anyway.

"Half the morning? And no leads in all that time?" That was Piper again. As if Noah and Emily weren't really trying. They were, but he'd left because he was mostly getting in her way. She was a wizard with the tech, obviously super smart, but there was an electric charge between them that made focusing on the actual work damn near impossible. He'd spent most of his time trying to talk himself out of "accidentally" touching her.

Of course, he didn't want to report *that* to his siblings.

"There's a lot of data," Noah tried. "It's not like Emily's dragging her feet on this. You don't know this girl—"

"And you *do?*" Piper's look of surprise was genuine this time, and it flushed embarrassment through Noah. He was the youngest, used to having his judgment always questioned by his older brother and sister. And after allowing himself to be duped by the Colonel once again... and landing in the experimental cages because of it... the last thing Noah wanted was to be overly trusting. Of anyone. Or to make a stupid choice, especially when shifter lives were on the line.

The accusation hung between all three of them.

Noah put up both hands. "Okay, so I don't really know her. But I did check out her background, and it's freaky clean. Not so much as a parking ticket or overdue library book. But maybe you're right—maybe the sweetness and innocence are all an act, and I'm an idiot who can't judge people. It's possible." *Not likely,* he thought to himself, but he sure didn't want to get caught with his pants down on this. "All the more reason for me to stay on the case. She no doubt thinks she has me fooled at this point. So she'll be more likely to slip up if she's really the mole."

Piper gave him a pinched look, like she wasn't buying this bullshit either, but Daniel was nodding. He always was the easier one to lie to, being the straight arrow in the family. *Dad's favorite.* Noah knew Daniel had been instrumental in stopping their father, not to mention taking a personal interest in keeping dear-old-Dad behind bars in a military prison, but old habits died hard—both in Daniel's presumption that he was always right, and Noah's chafing against being bossed around by him.

"All right," Daniel said as if that settled it. "Watch her for now. But we need access to WildLove's database to do our own analysis."

"I'll work it," Noah said roughly.

Piper was still appraising him. "Either *you're* being emotionally manipulated in this… or she will be by the time you're done. I hope for your sake, Noah, that it's not you."

Noah sighed. "Or maybe we'll just work together and find the bad guy."

"That's an option, too." But she didn't look like she believed it.

Noah loved his sister more than anyone else in this crazy, fucked-up world—she was the one responsible for getting him out of the cage he managed to get himself locked away in—so he knew she was just looking out for him. It still rankled, though.

"I'll try not to get my heart completely obliterated or, you know, become actually dead." He said it in that soft voice he saved just for her. It was the voice that got them through all the hard times when they were kids—the one that said, *I know you care. I love you, too.* Those weren't words the three of them ever said out loud, but they were known anyway.

"Now you're talking," Piper said, but there was a shine in her eyes. She pulled him into a rough hug and then shoved him away. Then she shocked him by actually wiping at her eyes. "Damn hormones."

Noah grinned. "Hey, that's my future niece or nephew you're cursing at! You're going to have to clean up your language before the baby comes, young lady."

"Fuck you."

Noah burst out laughing, and it felt damn good to release the tension.

Daniel just shook his head.

Right then, Jace River, Piper's mate and husband, waved to her through the living room window, beckoning her.

She gave him a nod, then said to Noah and Daniel, "My hot husband needs me. See you losers later." She headed for the front door.

"You're already pregnant, Piper!" Noah called after her with a laugh. "You can stop having sex every five minutes now!"

She threw him a look like he was insane and disappeared into the safehouse.

He was still chuckling in her wake, but Daniel's serious look killed all his smiles.

"I wanted to talk to you, Noah," he said.

Oh shit. This couldn't be good. "Yeah?"

"How are you doing?" Daniel asked, his voice grave.

Damn. This was about the experiments. "Great! Better than Jimmy, I imagine. How's that guy doing?"

Daniel scowled at his dodge. "He's fine. Lost a lot of blood. Concussion. Nothing he won't heal from by the end of the day."

"That's good to hear," Noah said lightly. "Maybe I should go say *hi* and give him some moral support—"

"Noah." His brother had that look—the *I'm the big brother, you're going to listen to me* look.

Fuck. "Daniel, I'm fine."

"You're not *fine.* You underwent a whole shit-load of experimentation and washed out of the Army on a medical leave."

"I didn't *wash out,"* he ground out between his teeth. "That was just an excuse to come home. Thought you guys could use some help, for fuck's sake."

That excuse was at least plausible. There were multiple, active investigations going on related to the hate group's activities. His cousin Nova's pack had bagged one of the bad guys—a sick fuck who liked to make videos about dismembering wolves and had actually kidnapped her—but the Wolf Hunter was someone else. It was hard to tell if there were multiple people involved in the hate group or if it was just random vigilantes who were inspired by the Wolf Hunter's videos. Some of both, probably. Right now, Riverwise was focused on putting the WildLove bomber out of business. As a result, a lot of Riverwise business got done here at the safehouse, where everyone was, well, *safe.*

But Daniel obviously wasn't buying this idea that Noah had returned just to help out.

His brother narrowed his eyes. "You wouldn't voluntarily come within a hundred miles of the Colonel, not if you could avoid it," he said. "You're not fooling me, Noah. Something happened in Afghanistan. What is it?"

Noah sucked in a breath and avoided Daniel's piercing stare. "Nothing I can't handle." Which was true. He could keep his beast under control, shift when he needed to, just like when he demonstrated his wolf nature to Emily. He just didn't want anyone in the shifter community to know what he'd become. *A white wolf.* She was right about them being legend… only that legend was part of his family. His grandfather's generation, to be precise, where the beta who broke up the Wilding pack by fucking the alpha's mate was a white wolf. Only white wolves weren't really wolves at all… they were some kind of male witch. Bobby Wilding was the beta, and the secret family shame was that the five sons born to the alpha, Gary Wilding, might actually have been fathered by Bobby. Only no one knew for sure if any of them had.

Until now.

Noah was pretty damn sure his father, the Colonel,

was actually the son of the white wolf, Bobby Wilding. The Colonel was one of those five brothers who scattered to the winds and formed the sprawling Wilding packs. He also messed around with Noah's genetics with his experiments. Once Noah had returned to Afghanistan, it became abundantly clear that his genetic code had something from the white wolf buried deep inside it.

His grandfather was, in fact, Bobby Wilding—which was so fucked up, it wasn't funny. Because being a white wolf meant Noah wasn't a wolf at all, not really. And the things he could do, the things he'd discovered in Afghanistan… that shit needed to stay buried, just like the secret family shame that it was.

"Noah, I'm trying to help you," Daniel said, finally breaking the awkward silence between them.

"Don't need your help, bro," Noah said tightly. "How about you just leave me alone?"

Daniel just glared icily at him. Thankfully, that was interrupted by Piper re-emerging from the safehouse.

Noah gave her an overly wide smile. "Hey, sis, I thought you getting busy—"

The dead serious look on her face cut him off. "There's been another car bomb."

"What?" Daniel said, his face twisting up.

Dammit. "I was hoping we had the guy," Noah said.

"You better come inside." Piper disappeared back through the doorway.

Daniel grabbed his arm before he could follow his sister. "We're not done talking about this."

Noah wrenched his arm free. "Actually, we are." He strode toward the front door and hurried inside, where Jace, Piper, Jaxson, and several other wolves were gathered at the far end of the great room. It had been turned into a war room of sorts—maps of Seattle pinned to the wall, a bank of computers set up on tables to the side, pictures of the grisly aftermath of the car bombings, suspects, and other evidence. Jaxson, the alpha of the River pack and one of the River brothers who ran Riverwise, was nominally in charge of the operation, but everyone was pulling their weight.

Jaxson lifted his chin to acknowledge Noah striding up. "We've got a copycat."

"I thought we were keeping this quiet," Noah protested. "How can we have a copycat, if no one knows what's been happening?"

"Well, *someone* does," Jaxson replied. "How's it going at WildLove? Any leads?"

"Not yet." Noah grimaced. "In fact, they're completely shut down now. Are we sure this is a WildLove hookup?"

"Yeah," Jaxson said grimly. "Jared's on the scene—he was in the area—and the girl is freaking out. The shifter is in critical condition. The girl says she made the connection last week, originally planned a hookup last weekend, but it got rescheduled to this afternoon."

Shit. "So there could be more hookups out there, waiting to happen," Noah said, "even though WildLove's shut down. Previous connections who are just now getting together."

"Right," Jaxson said. "There have to be tons of connections out there that have already been made. I think we need to open WildLove up again but carefully control it. Stake out each and every hookup."

"There's no way we can do that," Jace spoke up. "There are too many of them. Plus, it's just too dangerous for the parties involved."

"Then find me a better solution," Jaxson said with a taut stare around at the gathered wolves.

Daniel spoke up. "If we shut WildLove down permanently, eventually the hookups will drop off."

Noah frowned. That wouldn't be the end of the

world, although it would mean Emily and her co-workers would be out of jobs. And there would be a lot of horny wolves not getting any action... also not a tragedy, not compared to people dying.

"Not fast enough," Piper said. "And what if people die in the meantime?"

She had a point.

Noah gave her a nod of support. "Besides, the hookups could just go underground. People will find each other another way, maybe on the other apps that are out there. Ones we won't have access to. Besides, we don't know for sure if it's the app that's leading the bomber, or *bombers,* to the couple, or if the humans are somehow involved."

"It has to be the app. There's no connection between the women that we've been able to find." Jaxson rubbed his hand over his face. "And I don't really think this is a copycat. Two *separate* lunatics don't randomly decide to car bomb hookups on WildLove, especially when it hasn't made the news. They have to be working together, probably part of the hate group."

Noah frowned. "You're probably right about that."

Jace added, "And if they're both part of the same organization, it's possible they can lead us to the Wolf

Hunter himself."

"Exactly," Jaxson said. "If we can catch this second guy, we can connect the two bombers and find the rest of the network."

"All right," Noah said with a sigh. "I'll head back to the agency. See if I can talk them into opening up WildLove again so we can try to entrap this second bomber."

Jaxson nodded. "Report back when you've got a plan for us."

"Copy that." Noah spun around and headed for the door.

Daniel tried to catch his eye on the way out, but ignoring his brother's pointed looks was a skill Noah had honed long ago. And besides, he'd much rather be back at the agency working with their hot lead programmer, trying to catch the bad guys, than hanging around the safehouse getting interrogated by his all-too-strident brother. And not just because Noah didn't want to spill his secrets. In a way, he loved Daniel just as much as he loved his sister, Piper, although he'd rather take a bullet than say that out loud. But Daniel didn't need to know the truth about their grandfather. He didn't need to know that all three of them—Noah, Piper, and Daniel—were descended from a white wolf.

It would tear his straight-laced brother apart.

CHAPTER 4

"No way! A wolf gave you his number?" Sophie asked with awe in her voice. She was Emily's best friend, a fellow programmer for WildLove and, at the moment, she was attacking her salad like it had committed a personal grievance against her. Then she leaned forward. "This is your chance, Emily. You've totally got to do this."

Emily shook her head and picked at her own lunch. It was her favorite chicken Caesar salad, the one she had every day, but her stomach had been a giant bundle of squirming anxiety all morning. She could hardly focus at all with a ridiculously sexy shifter looking over her shoulder. Eventually, Noah had gotten sick of her bumbling around and coming up with nothing from WildLove's masses of data. He left, saying he had to check in with his company, Riverwise, at some safe location they had in the mountains, but she was sure he was just frustrated at her lame inability to function around him. Once he was gone, she had been able to concentrate, but she still hadn't come up with anything that would explain how the car bomber knew she and Noah were having a hookup last night, much less where. All that data was in the secure chat room that she'd specifically designed to have ultra-tight security. Only the two WildLovers planning a hookup had access… and anyone inside the agency. Which once again pointed to a mole. Which made her stomach fist up into more knots.

"I don't know, Soph," Emily said, still poking at her food. "I don't think I can hook up with Noah now."

"What are you talking about?" Sophie stared at her like she was crazy… and she probably was for not instantly taking Noah up on his offer. "He's hot. He's already kissed you. He knows who you are and what you do—this is even better than a WildLove hookup. He's *given you his number,* for God's sake."

"That's just it." Emily sighed and gave up on her salad. She simply had no appetite. "It was supposed to be a one-night thing. Now that I know him, it's not the same."

"Why not? You could still agree that it's just temporary." She flicked her fork in the air like it was a whip. "Go ride some wild wolf for a night, then move on and find a real boyfriend. One who will bring you pizza and a movie when you feel like crap, like my William." That was Sophie's boyfriend—they nerded-out together big time, going to cons, gaming, the works. Sophie tamed her fork and used it on her salad again. "You don't want a relationship with a shifter, anyway—they've got too many problems. That whole hate group thing with people trying to blow them up. Besides, there are good *human* men out there, Emily, you just need to get over your, you know, issues." She leaned forward again. "This could be really good for you, Em. It's what you need."

Her best friend was probably right about that—she usually was. And she knew more about Emily than anyone else on the planet, including Emily's useless family. The two of them had been roommates all through college, and Emily brought her on board at Seattle Shifters as soon as she'd scored the lead programmer position. Sophie was cool, normal, and super kind—and she knew all about Emily's past. Emily should listen to her, but her gut was saying *run away* with the volume of an eighteen-wheeler bearing down on her at sixty miles an hour.

She put down her fork and bunched up her napkin, twisting it in her hands. "I thought being with a shifter for one night would get me over the past. But now, everything's messed up."

"I still wish you would have told me about this hookup plan of yours," Sophie said with a scowl. "Regardless of your complete lack of faith in me as a true friend, the plan itself is brilliance. And for the record, I would've totally supported you, had I known. This is exactly what you need to move past what happened with your uncle. It's been five years, Em. It's time. Even your therapist would agree with me."

"I gave up on the therapist last year. Wasn't going anywhere." The truth was, Emily had buried herself in her work instead… and an obsession with shifters. It seemed like the right thing to do at the time—she couldn't keep going back to her therapist, week after week, with no sign of progress. And really, no desire to change anything in her safe, comfortable life.

"Yeah, I figured." Sophie jabbed her fork at Emily again. "And I think *that* was a mistake, too. But I'm telling you, none of that matters now. You've got this guy who wants to be with you. And he's a good guy, right?"

A hot trickling feeling went through Emily. "He's amazing, Soph. You don't even know. Brave and selfless, and he's got this cute sense of humor... he's really everything I could've hoped for in a one-time, super-hot romantic fling."

Sophie held her hands up. "See? That's what I'm saying. It's the WildLove motto—*Wild For a Night*—come to life. You know you'll be safe, and these guys are hunkalicious—if I didn't have my William, I'd be all over test driving some wolf myself."

Emily's mouth dropped open. "It's totally against the rules, Soph!"

"You're kidding me right?" She smirked. "Come on, Em. You don't even have to break the rules to be with him now—he gave you his number! He's safe and wonderful. Perfect for you. I don't see the problem."

Emily groaned in frustration. "The problem is that I'm not a wolf."

Sophie narrowed her eyes. "If you were a wolf, you'd have clawed the fuck out of that asshole uncle of yours. And you wouldn't even be in this situation. Your point is moot."

Emily just squeezed her eyes shut and shook her head.

But Sophie wasn't giving up. "Besides, I don't understand why that makes any difference. So, you're human—so what? If WildLove has proven anything, it's that humans and shifters will get it on, all day long—and have a hell of a good time doing it. Why can't you be part of that? You, more than anyone else I know, deserves to get laid by a hot shifter."

Emily opened her eyes but kept them fixed on her plate. "I don't want to get hurt, Soph," she said softly.

Sophie hesitated, then said, "I thought you believed shifters were the good guys. That's the whole idea, right? Shifters are *safe.*"

"It's not that." Emily peered up. "It's because it's temporary. And I'm human. Even if Noah wanted more than one night…" Her eyes glazed over, just thinking about it. Someone like Noah—strong and sexy and brave? Having him for real was an impossible dream. She sucked in a breath and blew it out. "He'll take a mate someday. A *shifter* mate. He won't want anything to do with me after one roll in the sheets. Two at the outside."

Sophie put down her fork and threw both hands in the air. "I thought that's what you *wanted!*"

"I've spent all of a couple hours with him, Soph, and I'm already… let's just say, I can already feel the heartbreak coming. And I don't know if I can withstand it. It would have been so much easier if we'd just done it at the motel. I have to just forget about Noah that way. Once WildLove is back online, maybe I'll try again. I'll study the database and find the perfect wolf to be my dream one night stand."

Sophie just shook her head. "You're going to regret this."

Emily picked up her fork again and took her frustrations out on her salad. "Probably."

Her best friend pulled in a breath and, mercifully, changed subjects. "How long do you think we're going to be shut down?"

"I don't know." Emily dropped her fork again, disgusted. "I'm doing everything I can. But if we don't figure out this thing soon, I don't see how WildLove can keep going, honestly. I mean, as long as there's a danger to shifters, we can't in good conscience open it up again."

"*Shit.*" Sophie grimaced. "What about our jobs?"

Emily just shrugged one shoulder. "These are people's lives were talking about, Soph."

"Yeah, I know." But she worried at her lip with her teeth.

Emily pointed a finger at her. "And you need to keep all this quiet. If we've got a mole at the agency, I don't want to give them a head's up that I'm hunting for them. And don't feed any of the rumors I'm sure are running all around the office today." She sighed and pushed back from her seat, fumbling to get her phone and purse together. "I should get back to work. It's hard for me to do anything when Noah's around—my body goes into Lust Overdrive Mode just being in the same airspace. I should get stuff done now, in case he comes back."

Sophie leaned back and crossed her arms. "I stand by my original point on this issue—you should jump that wolf as long as the offer is still open."

Emily huffed a small, mirthless laugh. "It's probably already expired. I'll catch you later."

She left her friend to finish her meal, but she could feel her worried stare on her back all the way out. Sophie really was the best. She just didn't understand what a mess the inside of Emily's head was... and how torn up she was already feeling, both terrified and hopeful that

Noah Wilding might have returned to the office while she was out at lunch. Any more involvement, and she would tumble into a deep, dark place when he inevitably broke it off.

And that wasn't something she could afford to do.

CHAPTER 5

"I'm sure Emily can find a way to make it work," Noah said.

He was back in the CEO's office of Seattle Shifters, arguing with Marjorie about the need to open up WildLove again.

"I'm sure she can," Marjorie said grimly. "I'm just not sure it's wise." But then she tapped something into her phone, so Noah held his next attempt to convince her at bay. After a moment, she said, "Emily, could you please come to my office? Thank you." She hung up.

A small tightness he didn't expect, deep in his gut, danced up and smacked him in the face. There was no denying he was attracted to Emily, but this was something more—a tingly anticipation that had been building ever since he left the safehouse. Even his wolf had perked up at the idea of seeing her again, and that caught him off-guard—Emily was *human*. His inner beast shouldn't be reacting to her like this.

Noah shoved that aside. "We both want the same thing here, Marjorie," he said, pouring on all the charm he possessed with an earnest look and a small smile. "To clear out this threat and get WildLove back in business."

She cocked her head to the side. "Don't bat those pretty eyes at me, Noah Wilding," she said with fake admonishment. "Save that kind of thing for Emily."

He blinked and, astonishingly, felt heat rising in his cheeks. Was it that obvious he was attracted to Emily? Or was Marjorie just trying to get them together for her own match-making reasons? He prayed she was still in the dark about their almost-hookup—Emily had been adamant about keeping that secret. Which had given him the perfect opportunity to slip her his number. After all, her boss was practically shoving them together. Was it wise to hook up with her while working this job with the agency? Um… no. Would that stop him? Probably not.

As he stumbled for something to say that wouldn't make his thoughts completely transparent, Emily scurried into the room.

"Oh!" she said, pulling up short, obviously surprised to see him. "You're… back." She tugged at her t-shirt, which said *Will Write Code For Coffee*. His wolf gave a small growl of appreciation for the way it hugged her chest. Noah whipped his gaze up to her face, afraid of being caught ogling, especially with Marjorie's keen-eyed attention on him.

"Hey," he said, rather lamely, then forced his voice to sound at least a little professional. "Tell your boss it would be no problem to work some programming magic to open up WildLove again."

She frowned and took two more steps into the office, coming to stand equidistant between them. "I thought it wasn't safe?" She looked to her boss.

"That's what I'm saying." Marjorie gestured to him. "But Captain America here thinks he can catch the bad guys better if we're live."

Emily turned her pretty frown on him. "I thought you had already captured the bomber."

Noah grimaced. "There was a second bombing just an

hour ago."

"What?" Emily's already pale skin lost even more color. "Is the shifter all right?"

There was that feeling again, deep inside, stirred around by her concern. "Yes."

Her obvious relief was quickly followed by a cute scrunching up of her nose. "It must have been a prior contact."

"Yeah." Of course, she would figure that out right away. Noah had only spent a couple hours with Emily, but it was obvious she was crazy smart—that was part of what drew him to her, too. He edged closer. "The two of them were matched by WildLove last week."

She scowled and dropped her gaze to the floor. "Of course. The average time from swipe to message is less than an hour. From message to chat room connection even less. But from there, the data's all over the map. Hookups can be arranged within minutes, and the actual meet within an hour. Or it could be days. Or a week. All depends on schedules, day of contact, whether it's coffee or…" She looked up at him with those clear blue eyes blazing. "There are hundreds of people still at risk. This is not good."

He nodded. "Which is exactly why we need to activate

some kind of dragnet to pull in this second bomber—and whoever else is involved—before anyone else gets hurt."

She was nodding. "If there are two bombers, then there are probably more. We need to find the whole group. And shut them down." The fierceness in her voice made that spot low in his gut tighten again. She was unbelievably cute like this, a whip-smart kitten in angry, problem-solving mode. And her protectiveness was just turning him on more.

Stay on task, Wilding. It didn't help that she smelled of freshly-scrubbed skin and lavender soap, no perfume of any kind, just like this morning. And the night before. He forced himself to look away before it was obvious he wanted to haul her back to that breakroom and kiss her for real.

"See?" he said to Marjorie.

Her lips were pursed as she examined Emily. "What can we do, Em? I trust you more than anyone in the company on this. And you know this system better than any other programmer. What can we do to keep everyone safe but still lure this guy in and catch him?"

Noah swung back to look at her, trying to keep his face schooled and his thoughts on task. She was like a demon on the trail of some idea—he could tell by the way she wrinkled her brow, thinking furiously, so he kept quiet.

"We could…" She stopped to lick her lips, and that wasn't helping with him staying on task. "We could re-route all the messaging," she said, tentatively, then gaining steam. "Have it go through a central account that we monitor. Cut the shifters out of it entirely—send their messages to a holding pen while we sort this out. They're the targets, and we can't have them exposed to any more risk. But we'll let the human requests go through, in case they're part of the setup."

Noah frowned. "We haven't found any connection between the humans and the bomber we have in custody."

Emily stared at the floor. "If I could just figure out how they're getting access…" She was biting her lip again, and his wolf was paying *far* too much attention to that.

Noah gave Marjorie an apologetic look. "It could be someone inside WildLove." He waited for Emily to react to that, but she was still chewing her lip and staring at the floor.

"That's still a possibility," Marjorie said. "I hate to think it, but—"

"Hang on!" Emily's hands jumped in the air like she was stopping traffic. "I've got it." She took a breath, but her eyes were blazing again. "I thought whoever these people were, that they had to have accessed the database with everyone's real names and phone numbers, then hacked the phones—so I was looking for loopholes in that system—but that's not it at all. Otherwise, they wouldn't be restricted to attacking *during the hookup*. That must be the only information they have. Which means they have to be hacking the messaging system. It's the only way they could know when the WildLovers are meeting. But whoever they've got hacking for them is *good*, really good, because they're not leaving any traces afterward. It could be someone inside the agency, but anyone on the inside would have access to the *entire* database. Maybe someone is unknowingly giving them access just to the message system. Whoever it is, whether it's coming from inside the agency or not, I'll need to catch them in the act."

"By making WildLove active again?" Noah asked hopefully.

Her face was very serious. "Yes. But we have to be careful, all set up and monitored by us. We'll set the trap, and as soon as the bomber takes the bait, I should be able to trace them and see how they're getting in. Then I can block them to prevent it from happening again."

"But then how do we catch them?" Noah asked, frowning. It was good to shut down whatever security hole WildLove had, but they needed to catch the bad guys as well. Not to mention this might lead them to the Wolf Hunter.

"The same way as before—a hookup that's really a setup. Only this time, all the interactions will go through us. There'll be no actual hookups until the bad guy hacks into one of our fake message exchanges. Once we see he's tracking us, we'll stage a hookup and catch him when he shows up to plant the bomb."

"Sounds brilliant to me," Noah said with a grin, throwing a glance to Marjorie.

She was scowling at both of them but relented after a moment. "No WildLovers at risk?" she asked Emily.

"Nope," she said with confidence. "Just the Riverwise security guys waiting to take down the bomber."

"All right, then." Marjorie waved them out of her office. "Get going on this. I want the messages intercepted as soon as you can, before any more of our WildLovers can get hurt."

"Yes, Ma'am!" Emily had a shine in her eyes as she

spun to hurry out of Marjorie's office.

"Thank you," Noah said to Marjorie before hustling after Emily. She was hauling ass back to her cubicle, and by the time he caught up to her, she was already in her seat, pulling up screens of information that could be hieroglyphics for all he could tell.

"God, why didn't I think of this *before,*" she muttered, but it seemed mostly to herself.

He put a hand on her shoulder but jerked it back when she jumped.

She gave him an apologetic look. "Sorry. Just… tense." She grabbed her mug of coffee emblazoned with *Coffee is My Boyfriend*, took a nervous sip, then set it down again.

He frowned. "I just wanted to help. But if you'd rather I left…" He hoped she would say no to that, but she was back to that twitchiness she had before, at the motel. It tugged at something deep inside him. There was something wrong, something closed-up and hurting inside her, and it bothered him. *A lot.*

She dropped her shoulders from their hiked-up position and seemed to relax a little. "No, sorry, I'm just… weird. Ignore me. And please stay. I'll need your help for part of this."

Noah dragged a chair over to sit next to her, then gestured to the screen. "I doubt I can help you much with this."

She scowled at the screen. "I can't believe I left some kind of security hole for these haters to waltz through! I wish you guys had come to me sooner. If I'd known, I could have—"

"Thank you," he said, interrupting whatever regret comment she was about to conjure. She did way too much of that—apologizing for being tense, for keeping whatever was bothering her locked inside. He was very familiar with that kind of thing—dark secrets his family kept under wraps while they slowly killed them from the inside out. He wasn't exactly great at the whole *understand your feelings* thing, but he was working on it—he had to, in order to control his beast. It was way more powerful than it used to be, and he couldn't afford to lose his grip on it.

"Thank you for what?" Emily asked, turning to him with wide eyes.

He smiled. "For caring about wolves so much."

She looked him straight in the eyes, and it was like she was seeing inside him. It wasn't a bad feeling... not at all.

"Shifters are better people than most humans," she said, a little breathless. "At least, as far as I can tell.

Generally speaking." That delightful blushing color was back in her pale cheeks. He held her gaze, and if she didn't look away, he was seriously tempted to follow that up with a kiss. But she dropped her gaze to the floor, then her keyboard, then back to her screen.

Avoiding him again.

"Evil comes in all shapes," Noah said quietly. "Right now, I'd like to catch this particular brand of evil that's bent on blowing up innocent people."

She nodded, eyes on the screen. "Right."

"So how can I help with that?"

That brought her attention back to him, but a grimace was marring her pretty face. "I guess I need you to hook up with another human."

He lifted his eyebrows. "I thought the hookup was just going to be fake." The only hookup he was interested in having in the near future was sitting in front of him with her hands nervously tapping the edge of her keyboard.

"We need the bomber to think it's real," she said, her face drawing down.

"So... we have to set up a real meetup, but I don't have to actually sleep with the person." He didn't like what she was saying... and he liked the look on her face even less.

She shrugged one shoulder and turned back to the screen, fingers flying across the keyboard. "You didn't have to sleep with them before."

True. Dammit. But back then he had no reason *not* to, and he had every reason to make it *look* real, in case the human was involved in the setup. Or just to buy time for the bomber. But, of course, Emily had already figured all that out, including the fact that she wasn't the first WildLove hookup he'd had. "I'm kind of hoping I won't have to do that again."

Her shoulders twitched, but she didn't say anything. It took him a moment to piece together what she was thinking: that he regretted the almost-hookup with *her.*

Noah reached a hand over to touch her wrist.

Her fingers froze mid-stroke, and she slowly looked at him.

He stared her straight in the eyes. "I just gave my number to a girl. I'm hoping she might call. I don't want to get involved with anyone else, in case that happens." He didn't think he could be any more plain about what he meant.

Her eyes went a little wider, then she blinked several times and turned back to her screen before speaking again. "I guess... I guess you wouldn't have to go through with the hookup. If you didn't want to."

"Maybe *you* could be my hookup."

She whipped a look to him then wrenched it back to the screen. "Um... yeah... maybe we could work it that way. It's probably better if everyone involved knows what's happening. Plus that way your hookup won't be surprised when you don't exactly match your profile picture." She swallowed, but this time, her nervousness just made him smile. Because he was pretty sure she wanted it as much as he did, even if she wasn't coming out and saying it.

"Exactly," he said, scooting his chair closer to peer over her shoulder. "So, tell me how this is going to work."

She quickly glanced at him, right at her back, then leaned over to pull a laptop out of one of her desk drawers. "You'll need this." Then she was back at her keyboard. "I'll reroute the message system so that anything that comes from actual WildLovers goes to a holding pen but pings us that there's activity. If it's a shifter messaging a human, then you're on, Noah."

"I get to be the shifter?" he asked with a grin, catching on to how this game would be played.

"And I'll be the human," she said with a small smile. "We'll have to chat like we're really setting up a hookup, but it will all be fake. I'll be monitoring on my screen, see if there are any real-time breaches of security. Once there is, then that hookup will be the setup."

"So…" Noah's grin just grew. "I get to flirt with you online, under multiple names, agreeing to a bunch of different hookups… but I only get to go to one for real. With you."

"Well, yeah." She was blushing again, and his heart rate kicked up a notched. "Except, you know, we'll actually be conducting a sting operation."

He leaned forward. "How about after the op? Are you busy then? Or should I wait to ask once we're alone in a motel room again?" He really couldn't contain his smirk.

She shoved him back, but even with her little hands, he could tell she didn't mean it. "We have to catch a bad guy first."

"Deal!" Noah opened the laptop she had given him.

This was absolutely the best job he'd ever had.

CHAPTER 6

BRIAN: Hey, Amy, your picture is so hot, it burned out my phone.

AMY: Seriously, does that line work on anyone?

BRIAN: Did it work on you?

AMY: No.

BRIAN: You owe me a new phone, then.

AMY: Okay… maybe.

BRIAN: Maybe a new phone? Or maybe your chat number?

AMY: 347-2290

Emily grinned at her screen and closed the messenger window, switching over to the secure chat board. She and Noah had been chatting for a couple hours, off and on, each time pretending to be a different set of WildLovers. All the real communication was shunted into a holding file—Emily would resurrect those messages once WildLove was truly live again—but each time a real person initiated a contact, Emily routed it to Noah, who took whatever crazy pickup line was used and ran with it. They agreed ahead of time they would eventually have her give her chat number and then arrange a hookup… but making it look real meant they'd spent hours flirting.

Which was somehow safer for her than in person.

She could actually breathe when Noah wasn't in the room heating her skin just by looking at her. Right now, he was safely back at his apartment somewhere in the city. It had taken a while to get everything set up on the servers, and he said he had some errands to run, so he'd taken the tricked-out laptop with him. It was well into the evening before they were "live" again—the messages came through on a special app she set up on his computer, and she was afraid he wouldn't notice the ping alert, but he must have been keeping a close watch because he'd replied almost instantly.

They'd been chatting ever since.

Noah's first message as "BRIAN" in the chat room lit up her screen.

BRIAN: Hey, sexy thing. I'm so glad you wanted to chat. I'd still like that new phone, though.

AMY: I thought you shifters were only interested in one thing from humans...

BRIAN: Hot sex, yes. Absolutely. Also technology. We shifters don't have access to much, what with living in the woods and hunting elk.

AMY: I hope you have a license for that.

BRIAN: Oh shit. You're a narc, aren't you?

AMY: Yes.

BRIAN: ...

AMY: Should I bring my handcuffs?

BRIAN: YES

AMY: Time and a place, hot stuff.

BRIAN: Are you wearing the uniform? Please wear the uniform.

AMY: Only if you're naughty.

BRIAN: I have been extraordinarily bad. Require lots

of… punishments.

AMY: How about in an hour?

She wasn't sure if that was enough time for Riverwise to set up the sting, but it would be suspicious if every hookup were at the same relative time, not to mention location, so there was a bit of art in this part of the arrangement. Noah knew what the Riverwise guys were ready for—she'd let him have the final say on the details. Meanwhile, she carefully monitored all the data flows, looking for traces that they'd been tapped by the bomber… but so far nothing.

BRIAN: I'm watching my favorite movie, *Sleepless in Seattle*. How about two hours? I don't want to miss the ending.

AMY: You're putting me off for a movie?

BRIAN: It gets me in the mood.

AMY: You're kind of sentimental for a hot shifter guy, aren't you?

BRIAN: Yes. Also naughty and very good at picking locks. Two hours at the Skylark motel? Message me the room when you get there?

AMY: I'll have extra handcuffs ready.

Emily waited, checked the data streams, but still nothing. It was possible the message board was being hacked without her realizing it, but she didn't think so. Plus all the chats were flushed out of the less-secure buffers and sent to the more-secure archives after about five minutes of inactivity. There shouldn't be any security holes in the first place, but if there were, she should see the hack in the real-time buffers. Which was why she had to catch the hackers in the act. Even if they could erase their digital footprints, or somehow they got wiped when the data went to archive, the hackers couldn't avoid leaving a trace in real time. But after five minutes, there was still no sign of intrusion.

Emily logged out of the message board—going offline was her signal to Noah that the hackers hadn't taken the bait. That little hookup between AMY and BRIAN would just fade into the archives, one more fake hookup that would never happen in reality.

Although Noah seemed intent on hooking up with her for real, once all this was over.

That sent a shiver down low in Emily's belly. On one hand, it was a shiver of anticipation. On the other, she couldn't imagine actually going through with it. But each with chat message they closed out, she was both more desperate to take him to bed and more terrified it would break her heart. The safest thing would be to just stay friends. Maybe even flirty friends.

Colleagues.

Right.

She didn't know how much of this flirting was real—well, she knew *none* of it was real, but she didn't know if Noah was enjoying it as much as she was. Most likely, he was just doing his job. That would make more sense than him lusting after her the way she was panting at the prospect of having him touch her... far more panting than she'd ever done for any other guy, even in her occasional fantasies about the cute programmer down the hall. Everything about Noah was just over-the-top perfect—he was a shifter, he was incredibly hot, and being a wolf, she *knew* she was safe with him. Plus he was smart and funny.

That last part was killing her. Because he was the kind of guy she actually might like to keep around... and Noah would never want her long-term. Although he'd definitely made it clear he wanted a short-term hookup. The question was: *why?* She couldn't really imagine. Supposedly, all guys were hot for any kind of sex anytime, and shifter libido was legendary. They were sex gods among men. But they were also ridiculously hot and could have any girl they wanted. So why bother with her? There was literally *nothing* about her that a sexy shifter like Noah couldn't get just as easily from AMY or SHELLY or APRIL… or any of the other profiles he'd flirted with tonight.

Her brain kept nagging at that and coming up frustrated.

Meanwhile, her screen pinged with another message coming in—this one was also from a male shifter initiating contact with a human female he had matched with. That was the typical profile. The shifters could have their pick of the women, generally speaking, but they were also looking for a fast hookup… so they usually made first contact when they were available, working their way through the list to see who would respond the fastest. Human females with any sense jumped right on that opportunity when it appeared… so Emily quickly routed NICK's message to Noah along with her response as TRISH to get things rolling and appearing normal.

NICK: Wow, your smile is making my wolf growl.
TRISH: Yeah?

Noah's first foray into the discussion came quickly…

NICK: Like you don't even know. Which is unusual… my inner beast typically only responds to other shifters. Are you sure you're not part wolf?

Of course, he knew she was human. But it made her heart thump anyway… why was he taking the message in this direction?

TRISH: Positive I'm not a wolf. But I love everything about them.
NICK: Have you ever been with a wolf before?

Emily felt her face heat up. Why was he asking this?

TRISH: No. First time. Is that okay? Does that turn you off?
NICK: The opposite. I can't wait to explore your wild side.

Her face was definitely ten degrees hotter than the room now.

TRISH: I guess you want my chat number, then?

NICK: I want a whole lot more than that, but I'll settle for the number.

TRISH: 347-2290

Emily's hands shook a little as she closed down the messenger and logged into the secure chat board again. Okay, maybe even *online* and *halfway across the city* wasn't enough distance to keep her from feeling the heat that Noah generated in her.

"NICK's" chat message lit up right away.

NICK: I have to be honest. I'm drooling at the thought of getting closer to you.

Gulp. Oh God, were they really going to do this? Message sex-talk? It wasn't like it didn't happen—she'd seen it get scorching hot online—but she'd never imagined doing it herself. Much less with a man she knew she'd see again sometime in the next twelve hours.

TRISH: Um... don't drool on the keyboard. Could cause problems.

So lame. She had no idea how to do this.

NICK: Can't help it. You're so damn sexy.

She should just cut to the chase with this, so they could move on to another, less aggressively sexy, persona. And she could go splash cold water on her face. Something.

TRISH: You're pretty hot yourself. Maybe we should hook up?
NICK: Maybe. Depends.

Wait... what? Noah wasn't supposed to play hard to get. What was he doing?

TRISH: Depends? On what?
NICK: On how long you can last. Are you up for a whole night? Are you well rested? Have you had your dinner? Because you're going to need your energy, sweet thing.

Oh God.

TRISH: I can handle whatever you've got in mind, wolf boy.

NICK: I'm not a BOY. And what I've got in mind starts with just my hands, all over your body, every place that can be touched. Then my mouth is going to taste you, inside and out. And when I'm finally inside you, believe me, you'll know just how much MAN I have to give. I want to feel every ripple of your orgasms like you're part of me.

Oh. My. God. Emily pushed away from her desk, her heart pounding and pushing hot blood throughout her body… and pooling it between her legs. How could she look him in the face the next time they met, now that he'd said those things? And what could she possibly say in return?

Her mouth was dry, and she swallowed hard. Then an off-tone ping sounded, and it took a moment in her panicked state to realize what it was: *the alert she'd set up for an intruder.*

She slammed back to the keyboard, opening a separate window to track the intrusion.

Yes! There he was, the hacker, lurking in the

background of their supposedly secure chat… he was just a surge in the data download that wasn't there a moment ago but was unmistakable now. She put a trace on it, even though she didn't expect that to turn up anything. More importantly… she had to set up the meet!

NICK: Are you there?

Oh shit.

TRISH: Yes! Damn… sorry… just overheating from your last message.
NICK: Thought maybe I scared you off.
TRISH: No. God no. Can't wait to feel your hands on me for real.
NICK: Yeah?

Shit. He didn't know this wasn't for real. Or maybe it was, but that part didn't matter right now. What mattered was getting the hookup set before their lurker gave up on them.

TRISH: Oh yeah. Just tell me when and where, and I'll be there. I'll keep going as long as you can.

NICK: Promises, promises.

TRISH: You're the one with all the teasing. How about you show me what you can do offline?

Dammit, Noah needed to hurry this along. Then she smacked her palm to her forehead—his phone! She snatched her phone off her desk and quickly searched for Noah's number. It took agonizingly long to find it. Meanwhile, "NICK" was still messaging her.

NICK: I'm not teasing. I'll make every fantasy you have about wolves come true.

She quickly typed…

TRISH: When and where?

Then she texted Noah on his personal phone, *Hacker is watching us.* It took a moment, but when he texted back, it was simple. *Copy that.* Then "NICK" messaged her again.

NICK: Are you ready now?
TRISH: Yes!

NICK: How about the Stryker Motel? One hour?

TRISH: Perfect!

NICK: Message me with your room when you arrive.

TRISH: Can't wait.

Then she logged out immediately—their signal that the meet was on. As soon as she did, the trace disappeared... and so did the hacker. Emily searched the archives, but there was no indication that he'd been there or anywhere else in the system. If she hadn't captured the feeds real-time, there would have been no evidence at all that something strange had happened on that particular chat.

But it had.

Her phone buzzed. It was a text from Noah. *We need to move fast. Need to get there before him.*

Copy that, she replied, then grabbed her stuff and ran for the elevator.

CHAPTER 7

"She's late. Something's wrong." Noah peered through the back window of the Riverwise pack van, scanning the streets darkened with rain and glistening with the city's night lights. The traffic was light but steady—this shady side of downtown never slept—but there was no sign of Emily's silver Prius. He'd given her the address of the liquor store where they were parked, but maybe her GPS wasn't working…

"You could text her again while she's driving," his

brother, Daniel, said from the driver's seat. "Because that was such a great idea the last two times."

"Something's wrong," Noah said again, his hand palming his phone in his pocket, itching to do exactly what his jerk brother was saying he shouldn't do.

"She's not even late. The meetup isn't for another fifteen minutes." Daniel climbed out of the driver's seat and joined him in the back of the van.

Noah glared at him. He shouldn't have said anything, just texted Emily like he wanted to. Now, Daniel's big-brother look of concern was all over him, and he couldn't do it without taking crap. Chatter in Noah's earbud distracted both of them for a moment—the rest of the pack was checking in from their stations around the motel. Two of them had rented rooms, posing as legit customers. The others had arrived surreptitiously, joining them or staking out spots in the darkened stairwell corners or parked at the IHOP next door. All told, they had a dozen Riverwise shifters ready to take the bomber down, if he showed. It should be more than enough.

But having Emily in the middle of it was making Noah unexpectedly nervous.

The chatter died down, and just as Daniel opened his mouth to say something—something Noah was sure he didn't want to hear—a silver Prius pulled up alongside the van.

"She's here." Noah pushed past his brother to slide open the van door.

Emily climbed out of the driver's seat, and her smile lit up when she saw him. It warmed him and flushed cool relief through him, all at the same time. Which was a fair description of the feelings she was stirring up in him—all conflicted and bothered. Ever since their chat had gotten hotter than he had planned, and then she'd pulled back from him, it had left him nervous. Afraid she thought he was only after sex from her... and then afraid that he actually wanted more.

He waved her into the van.

She looked Daniel over with wide eyes. "Hi," she said to him, but it was soft and a little breathy. Like she was shy, or maybe attracted to him. The flush of jealousy that surged up stunned Noah so badly, he fought for a moment to say anything at all.

"So, you're the famous *Emily-the-programmer*," Daniel said with a smirk, managing to be an asshole in less than ten words.

Emily's shyness disappeared. She lifted one eyebrow and looked to Noah. "Famous?"

Noah just shook his head. "Please don't listen to a thing my brother says. *Please.*"

"What?" Daniel's ridiculous look of innocence wasn't fooling anyone. "I'm just saying—"

"Don't." Noah glared a threat at him, then reached for Emily's hand and pulled her further into the van, away from Daniel. "Ignore him," he said softly. "Are you all right?"

She frowned. "Yeah, I'm fine. Why?"

"I just... nothing." He would explain about the chat later when they were alone. "Okay, here's the plan. Riverwise is already in place. They'll have eyes on you from the moment you enter the motel parking lot. You go ahead and check in, then message me the room number. I'll follow in about fifteen minutes, so it doesn't look like I was hanging out at the liquor store right around the corner."

"Sounds good." Emily glanced at Daniel, then back at Noah. "So then... what? We just wait?"

"We've been watching the place for the last half hour," Daniel said. "Two couples have checked in, but that's it. Unless the bomber miraculously got here before us, he hasn't shown yet. But when he does, we'll be waiting for him."

"But you don't know what he looks like," she protested.

Noah's stomach clenched. "No. Which is why I'll be straggling in. We want to give him plenty of time to get here and see me arrive. I'll keep my hood up, just in case he's downloaded the profile pix from the hookup."

"Are you sure that's wise?" she asked, her cute nose scrunching up. "I mean, what if he decides to just shoot you as you're getting out of the car?"

Noah worked to keep the smile off his face. She wasn't worried about herself walking into a sting operation to catch a bomber... she was worried about *him*. "I doubt he'll do that. It's much safer for him to wait, make sure I'm the right guy by going to the right room, then slip out of whatever cover he's keeping to plant the bomb on my car and slip away. He could be watching from across the street or the forest preserve behind the motel or any number of places. And he's sure to be extra careful this time because we've already caught his co-conspirator. He might even show up much later after he's sure we're... *indisposed* inside the room."

She lifted both eyebrows. He prayed she wouldn't mention any of their sexy chat-talk in front of Daniel. But she just said, "Okay. That sounds, well, reasonable, at least." She glanced at her phone. "I better go."

"Okay." Noah wanted to hug her or reassure her or... something. Instead, he just said, "Be careful."

She smiled, and he swore it lit up the inside of the van.

Damn, he was in trouble with this girl. How did that happen so quickly? It must have been the hours they spent online, talking and flirting and spilling little details about their lives.

He watched her climb out of the van and back into her Prius. Just like the first time they met, he was almost hoping the bad guy wouldn't show, or at least would take his time, just so Noah could be alone with Emily in the motel room. Only this time, he just wanted to talk. Find out how much of those chats were *her* and how much were a front. See if he really threw her with the sexy talk or not. And, okay, maybe kiss her as well.

So much trouble.

"You like this girl." Daniel's voice was drenched in disapproval, as usual.

Noah closed his eyes, reining in the urge to just have it out, right here, in the van. Preferably with claws and fangs. "That's not a crime, you know."

"She's human." Daniel was still aghast.

"I noticed." Noah forced out a breath, opened his

eyes, and turned to his brother. "It's not like I'm mate material, Daniel."

His face grew instantly serious. "You're talking about Afghanistan."

Noah sighed. Fifteen minutes stuck in a van with his brother, and already they were on the worst possible topic. "Yes, because of what happened in Afghanistan. And the cages."

Daniel's eyes narrowed. "The experiments affected you." He was guessing, but it wasn't a wild leap.

"Let's just say, I'm not the wolf you grew up with."

"*Noah.*" For once, his brother seemed genuinely distressed. Which was somehow worse than all the condescension and arrogance. Because he had to believe there was something really, seriously wrong with his brother to turn this kind of soft.

The temptation to tell Daniel about their grandfather, the white wolf of disgrace, was overwhelming... it would knock him back on his arrogant ass to know he was descended from a lying, cheating male witch. But Noah couldn't bring himself to do it.

Some secrets really should stay buried.

"Look, I'm fine, honest," Noah said. "You remember when Owen was afraid to shift after he'd been in the cages for a year? Because he didn't know what kind of beast he would be?"

Daniel nodded. That story had made the rounds through Riverwise after Owen finally shifted and was revealed to be a white wolf with freakishly large, razor-sharp claws.

"Well, it's something like that—monster claws, a different kind of wolf than I used to be—but I can control it. My new wolf form came out when I was in Afghanistan, freaked the hell out of me, and I came home. But I'm fine now—I've got it under control." Not the entire truth, but maybe enough to keep Daniel off his back about it.

His brother nodded. "That's why you think you're…" He grimaced.

"A freak? Yes. Just say it, Daniel."

"That's not what I meant!" His brother's face darkened. "I was going to say that's why you think you're not mate material."

"That too." Noah scowled at him.

"But that's not necessarily true—"

"*Come on,* bro! Don't patronize me. We both know there aren't enough female wolves to go around, not by a long shot, and there aren't going to be any lining up to mate with someone who's a genetic freak." Not to mention that he wasn't fully a wolf… even if there were a female shifter interested in him, he'd have to tell her the truth. It was only fair. And no reasonable girl would want to risk having half-witch pups. Hell, any girl who did, he probably wouldn't want, just because that would be crazy.

"Don't give up on this!" Daniel looked distraught. "Owen found a mate—"

"That was luck, man, and you know it."

"It could happen for you. Don't throw away—"

"Okay, *look.*" Noah got in his brother's face. "I'm making my own path here, Daniel. And you do *not* get a vote on what it's going to be."

Daniel pressed his lips into a tight line, but Noah really didn't give a fuck at this point what his brother thought of him. And if Noah wanted to be with a human, not just for a night, but maybe for longer—

His phone buzzed.

It was the WildLove chatroom app. *Room 19,* Emily's message said.

Fuck waiting around for fifteen minutes. "We're in Room 19," Noah said to his brother. "Time for me to go."

Daniel held up his hands to stop him. "I thought you

were waiting."

"I'll take the scenic route." Noah pushed past him, threw open the door of the van, and hopped out. Then he slammed the door in Daniel's face for good measure. His car was on the far side of the van, and by the time he reached it, the boiling anger inside him was surging up his wolf. He breathed through his teeth, willing his wolf to stay calm, promising him that they were going to see Emily in just a few short minutes.

It worked. He wasn't even halfway around the scenic route to the motel before he was calm again… at least, as calm as he got with the prospect of seeing her looming ahead.

That part he really didn't understand. It was like his wolf was drawn to her for some reason. Given his wolf was only half-wolf—the other half being witch, plus whatever altered stuff the genetic experiments threw in there—he wasn't sure what any of it meant. All he knew was he couldn't wait to see her. And all the disparate parts of himself settled down and pulled together in an effort to make that happen.

There were several cars in the motel parking lot, but no people. Noah parked well away from Emily's silver Prius, as well as Room Nineteen, just in case the bomber managed to set something off and blow up his car—he didn't want Emily or her car getting caught in the crossfire. Then he jogged up to the door. It was on the first level this time, and he took a moment, catching his breath and hopefully giving the potential bomber a good long chance to see him before he knocked.

Emily opened the door right away. She was still wearing her black t-shirt and jeans getup from the office, which made sense. She had probably come straight from there, whereas Noah had been doing their online chatting from his apartment... where he wouldn't be tempted to follow up those sexy chats with multiple attempts at a kiss. But now that they were here...

"Hi, Trish!" Noah said, still standing outside the door, playing the role, in case the bomber was watching. "I'm Nick. From WildLove."

"Hey, Nick." Emily couldn't quite contain her smile, and it practically forced one onto his face. "Nice to meet you. Come on in." She stepped back and held the door wide for him.

"You're just as sexy as your profile picture," Noah said, a parting comment for the potential bomber outside.

Emily closed the door and turned to him. She folded

her arms across her chest and shook her head, giving him a skeptical look. "Is that right? Because, as I recall, Trish is a heck of a lot taller and skinnier than I am."

Was she really walking him right back into the sexy talk? Because he was *so* ready to pick up where they left off.

"I happen to like shorter with more curves." He closed the couple feet between them, and he could tell by the way her eyes widened, that she didn't expect it. He let his gaze travel down to where her t-shirt hugged her chest, then back up to her eyes. "And what you have under there looks very tempting to me."

Her mouth went a little slack with surprise, and her cheeks pinked up right away. Man, she was pretty when she blushed. It brought out that innocent-kitten look to her wide blue eyes and creamy-pale skin. He eased closer, nudging her toward the door without touching her. Yet.

"Um… okay," she said, and her voice hiked up a little. "You realize we're not in chat anymore, right?"

His heart sank a little with that, but he didn't give up. He pressed a hand against the door, next to her head, because by this time, she was backed all the way up against it. Her arms were still locked, protectively, across her chest.

He looked straight into her eyes. "I was hoping at least some of it was real. It felt real to me."

She visibly swallowed. "Yeah. Me too," she whispered.

Yes. He leaned in closer. "I've never done that before. Talked like that in chat, I mean. Did I..." He licked his lips because suddenly his mouth was dry with nerves. "Did I scare you off? I kind of got carried away."

"No," she breathed. He was close enough that he could feel the heat of it. "Well... it *was* a little overwhelming."

"I'm sorry." He leaned in close enough to kiss but didn't. God, he wanted to. "And I don't want you to think that's all I want. That I'm just trying to get you in bed. Because it's not just that for me."

She blinked. "It's not?"

He eased back a little—any closer, and he *would* be kissing her, and that wouldn't help in making his point. "You're smart and funny as hell. And you're taking all kinds of crazy chances here, just to help shifters... when you're not even one yourself. And you... you *care*, Emily, in a big-hearted kind of way that stirs me around. So, *no*, it's not just your smokin' hot body that I want."

Her eyes were wide, and her lips parted, and he could scent her arousal... which was all he needed to press forward.

"Not that I don't want that, too. Don't get me wrong." He let his gaze rake down the smooth curve of her neck. He had to shut his mouth to keep in the drool again. He looked back into her eyes. "We're here, in a motel room, alone, *again*... and believe me, I'd really like to take off your clothes. And mine. Unfortunately, the bad guy could show up any moment."

"That's really unfortunate." She was whispering again.

"It is. But there's a lot we can do with our clothes still on."

Her breathing hitched. "Yeah?"

"Definitely." He placed his second hand on the door next to her head. There were only inches between them. "If you'll let me."

He was so close he could feel her chest heave against his as she labored to breathe. "I'll let you."

He managed not to moan with those words, just leaned forward and gently pressed his lips to hers. They were so soft... his hand was in her silky hair before he knew it, his other one around her waist, pulling her close. He wanted her to feel more than just his growling lust for her, but he couldn't help drawing her deeper into the kiss by crushing her to him. And his quickly growing erection was making that lust plain enough. She practically melted into him, her body hot against his through her thin t-shirt, his tongue deep inside her mouth, tasting and seeking and warring with hers. She was so short, her head had to tip back to kiss him. He slipped his mouth from hers, traveling wet kisses down her jaw and nipping at the tender skin of her neck. The moan that came from her throat reminded him that he wasn't making anywhere near enough use of his hands. He slid the one at her back down to caress her firm, little bottom, while the other brushed the side of her breast through her shirt.

"God, Emily," he panted between kisses, working his way back up to her sweet mouth. He cupped her breast in his hand as soon as a sliver of space opened between them.

"Oh my God, yes," she said before he smothered her words with his kiss.

He pressed her against the door, not caring that she felt every bit of hardness he had for her—she should know how much she affected him—but he was starting to lose himself in this kiss. His hand slipped under her shirt. Her small fingers clawed at the bottom edge of his, working it up so she had access to his bare skin. He devoured her sweet scent with his mouth and deep pulls of breath across her skin—

His earbud squawked, making him jump.

"No, no, no!" "What the hell!" "Get him!" *"Shoot him!"* "Too far!"

Noah jerked back from the kiss, blinking fast. "Something's happening outside."

But Emily had heard it, too, looking toward the window to the parking lot, drawn closed with drapes. The shouts were audible through the thin walls of the motel.

"Noah, get clear of the door!" That was Daniel, his voice high and hysterical.

It froze Noah for a split second, slicing like ice through his veins... then he grabbed Emily's hand and yanked her away from the door.

"Go, go, go!" he shouted to her as he dragged her across the span of the room. She stumbled but caught herself, plus he had an iron grip on her. But there was nowhere for them to go, no rear exit, no door to another room... *just the bathroom.* "Get inside!" he yelled while shoving her through the door and toward the bathtub.

He barely got through the door to the tiny bathroom himself before the room blew.

CHAPTER 8

E mily could hardly breathe with Noah's weight on her, but that didn't concern her... what was freaking her out was that he wasn't moving, and he was *in his wolf form.*

Something had exploded in the motel room, probably the door, but Noah had hustled her into the tiny bathroom and down into the bathtub before it hit—and the shock from the blast had thrown him in after her. He must have hit the tiled walls hard, and with his head, because it had knocked him unconscious and now he lay, inert, on top of her. Somewhere in the process, he had shifted into his beautiful white wolf form… but that didn't make him any less heavy.

"Noah! Noah!" she whispered hoarsely in his ear, the fur of his face tickling hers. She wriggled out from under the bulk of his weight, trying to ease him gently to the floor of the tub while getting a better look at his head. She couldn't see any blood in all that snow-white fur, but his eyes were closed tight and his tongue lolled out of his open snout. "Noah, please wake up," she said, tears pricking her eyes as she gently shook him.

Shouts were coming from the room outside, and the air was thick with smoke and small, floating debris from the explosion, but Emily's focus was entirely on the beautiful, noble wolf who had just saved her life. She dug her hands into his fur, searching for a heartbeat, but it was impossible—as much as she knew about shifters, she didn't know anything about the anatomy of their wolf forms.

But someone else might.

"In here!" she shouted to whoever was outside in the room. "We're in here! We need help!"

A pounding of footsteps was followed by Daniel, Noah's brother, swinging around the corner and into the small room. "Noah?" he gasped then flew to their sides.

He looked in horror at Noah's wolf form, like he had never seen it before.

"He won't wake up," Emily said, her throat closing up. But even as the words came out of her mouth, Noah stirred in her arms. His eyes were still closed, but his muzzle leaned into her, rubbing against her arm. "Noah! Can you hear me?"

"I need a medic in here!" Daniel screamed at the men gathered at the door. One disappeared, calling for someone. Then Daniel turned back to Noah. "Noah, God... what's happened to you?"

Then a miracle occurred—or at least it felt that way to Emily—and Noah opened those clear-blue wolf eyes and looked straight up into her face.

"Noah?" Daniel's voice drew a growl out of the wolf in her arms, and suddenly, he shifted, leaving her holding a very naked, very gorgeous Noah in the bathtub.

"Oh, thank God," Daniel said, rocking back on his heels where he was crouched by the side of the tub, but Noah ignored him, his eyes still locked with hers.

She put one hand on his cheek, holding his head as gently as she could with the other. "Say something." She searched his face for a sign of injury.

He smiled. "You're beautiful." Then he touched her

face with his fingertips—they were cold, but at least they weren't shaking.

"Okay, you really did get a knock on the head," she said, blinking back the tears that had been threatening to fall.

"Noah, please tell me you're all right." That was Daniel again.

Noah grimaced at his brother. "I'm fine." Then he seemed to want to get up, to show Daniel he was okay, so Emily let him go, even though she thought standing up was a very bad idea. Noah worked his way up to his feet, but then wavered a little and braced his hand against the wall.

Daniel stood as well. "You're not fine. You need to have Jace take a look at you."

Noah peered down at Emily as she scrambled to stand as well. "Are you okay?" he asked her.

"Yeah." She gave a small smile. "I think I cushioned your fall."

Noah squeezed his eyes shut for a moment. "God, what was I thinking, bringing you into this?" Then he opened his eyes and turned to his brother. "Make sure she's okay, Daniel. *Please.*" Noah's hand was rubbing his head like it hurt.

Emily frowned, but before she could say anything, Daniel was reaching to help her out of the tub. "Let me see you," he said, raking his gaze over her, apparently checking for injuries. "Can you stand? Did you hit your head or bang up anything?"

"No," she said, stepping out of the tub and dropping his hand to smooth down her shirt. "I'm fine, really. Noah's the one who needs help."

"See?" Daniel asked him. "Will you listen to her and sit down, please?" His voice was rough, but Emily could tell there was really concern behind it.

"What I need is some pants," Noah said, but he eased down to sitting on the edge of the tub. His clothes were in a heap at the bottom. Daniel knelt down to scoop them up and hand them to his brother. He took them without a word and started pulling them on. Just as he was standing to zip up his pants, another wolf pushed through the onlookers at the door.

Emily recognized him as Jace River, one of the brothers who ran Riverwise.

Daniel gestured to Noah. "He got a knock on the head."

"I'm fine," Noah grumbled, but then winced. "Just a headache."

"Sit down," Jace said in a tone that said, *I'm your boss, don't even think about arguing with me.* Or possibly it was his alpha voice. It sent a shiver through Emily, regardless.

Noah sat on the edge of the tub again.

Jace pulled out a penlight from a small, black kit and flashed it across Noah's eyes. Then he held up two fingers.

"How many?" he asked.

"Two," Noah said.

"Blurred vision?"

"No, just the headache."

Jace felt around Noah's head, standing to inspect his scalp through the mess of brown hair. Noah winced a little, which just made Emily wind her arms tighter around her chest. God, she hoped he was okay.

Jace stood. "All right, you're going to be fine. That lump on your head looks like it's already shrinking. Which is pretty damn fast, Noah Wilding. You couldn't have been hurt too bad. I'm going to say no concussion unless your symptoms start to get worse."

"See?" Noah peered up at Daniel. Then he looked back to Jace. "Can you check Emily, make sure she's okay?"

Emily unlocked her arms and put her hands up. "I'm

really fine."

Jace smiled warmly at her. "It'll make him feel better if we're sure."

She gave him a small, awkward nod. Daniel helped Noah get dressed while Jace repeated the same questions and routine with the penlight.

"Any pain or twisted ankles?" he asked.

"No," she replied.

"Well, you two are damn lucky, that's all I have to say." Jace stuffed his penlight back in his black kit.

Noah was shaking his head as he pulled on his shoes. "That was too damn close." He turned to her. "Emily, I'm sorry. I should never have brought you into this. I don't know what the hell I was thinking."

"I'm okay," she protested.

But he just shook his head some more, then peered up at Jace. "What happened?"

"The bomber must have slipped in as part of the couple in Room Twenty-Four." Jace grimaced. "I can't believe we missed that ploy. It was so obvious. Anyway, the woman left first. We didn't think anything of it. Then the man left their room and headed toward the parking lot. We figured he was leaving as well, but then he stopped at your door. I swear to God, Noah, he only paused for a second. That's all the longer it took to plant whatever explosives he used." Jace hooked a thumb over his shoulder toward the room. "Damn near took out the entire room, though. And half of the neighboring ones on all sides. Which, thank God, were empty."

"Did you catch him?" Noah asked.

"No," Daniel said through gritted teeth. "We weren't even onto the fact that he did something until he started hauling ass toward the back of the motel. Then the door blew and everything went sideways. We went after him, of course, but the woman must have been waiting for him out back. He was gone by the time we could follow."

"Dammit." Noah ran both hands through his hair and stood. He looked a bit more steady this time, which trickled relief through Emily. "All right. I'm getting Emily out of here. When you guys have a plan for what to do next, call me."

Noah reached a hand for her, and it didn't even occur to her not to go with him. He took her by the elbow, pulling her close, then hooked an arm protectively over her shoulders. Holding her tight that way, he walked her out into the room.

It was a nightmare.

Most of the room was gone. The explosives took out

not just the door, but the entire front wall, half the side walls, and a good chunk of the ceiling. Emily could see all the way to the roof of the two-story motel. The bed was thrown against the wall of the bathroom, and there was nothing left of the sparse furniture but bits of floating dust and broken pieces on the floor. If she and Noah hadn't made it to the protection of the bathroom, plus had the extra shielding of the bed thrown against the wall, they would both be in pieces just like the splinters of wall and shreds of carpet left hanging in the wounded room.

She coughed on the dust that choked the air. Noah pulled her closer, holding her tight against him as they picked their way through the wreckage. She heard sirens in the distance. There was no way Riverwise could keep this quiet… nor should they. The world should know there were insane people out there trying to kill shifters and the humans who wanted to be with them.

She held onto Noah as they left the room.

Her Prius had a two by four beam lodged through the windshield, somehow thrown from the room to stab her baby car. A small sob escaped her.

"We'll have it fixed." Noah's voice was tight, and his arms around her tensed even more. "I promise you, we'll make it right."

She just nodded, unable to get words out. The car didn't mean anything to her, not really, it was just... it could have been *her* with a giant hole. Or Noah. Somehow seeing the car like that sunk it home even more. Tears started running down her cheeks. She tried to hold them in, but she just couldn't, not anymore.

Noah walked her toward the far end of the parking lot where his car was. On the way, one of the other shifters jogged up to them, asking Noah if he needed anything. He told them no, that he was taking her to his apartment, that they could find him there if they needed him. But that they were leaving. *Now.* Before the police showed up and detained them with all kinds of questions. She only vaguely noticed all this, as she focused on keeping her legs moving forward. A strange buzzing had taken up residence in her head, blurring out the sounds of sirens and shouting and the stares of people coming out of their rooms. Noah opened the car door and gently helped her into the front seat, then ran around the front to climb in.

The closing of his door snapped her out of her haze. "Are you sure you're okay to drive?" she asked.

He was gripping the steering wheel hard and staring straight ahead. "I wouldn't drive you anywhere, if I wasn't okay to drive, Emily." His voice was strained. Then he turned to her, and she could see the night lights sparkling in the shine in his eyes. His gaze roamed her face. "You're crying." His hands were suddenly on her face, wiping away the tears. "It's going to be okay, Emily, I swear. You're safe now."

She nodded, moving against his gentle touch. "I know. I'm just... I'll be fine." She wiped at the tears to try to reassure him.

But it just seemed to cause him pain. "I shouldn't have brought you here. I'm an idiot for involving you in this. It's not safe. None of this is safe. And it's not acceptable to me to endanger you in any way."

"I'm okay, I promise."

His eyes bored into hers. "Wolves can recover; you can't. We have extraordinary healing powers—"

"I know." She gave him a small smile. "It's the magic in your blood. It enhances your metabolic rate, giving you extraordinary strength, as well as speeding your blood clotting and normal recovery processes about ten-fold."

The tension dropped off his shoulders. He huffed a small laugh and gave her an even smaller smile. "Of course, you know." He lifted his hand to touch her face again, this time just gently stroking her cheek. "What you may not know is that my white wolf has even faster healing. I'm uniquely able to survive pretty much whatever the bombers want to throw at me. But you, my sweet Emily, are soft and delicately human. And I'm not risking you in anything like this ever again. I like you way, way too much to lose you. And I'd never forgive myself if anything ever happened to you. All right?"

She nodded and tried to hold back her smile, but failed. The strength of his concern, the fact that he cared about her at all, his determination to keep her safe… all of it warmed her in a way she could hardly keep inside.

Noah released her, turned on the car, and drove them away from the motel. They were quiet during the drive to his apartment. She didn't know what would happen when they got there, but she decided in that moment, that whatever happened, she would let it. *She almost died tonight.* That thought kept ringing through her head with each passing streetlight strobing her eyes. She didn't want to die like this—lonely and scared to have a relationship with a man because it might trigger that dark place she'd been in before. She wanted to *live her life…* in every way. Maybe this would be the first and last night she could spend with Noah Wilding. Maybe her heart would get broken in the process. But she would be *living* for once in her life—with all the joy and pain and sorrows that went with that. Life held no promises, no guarantees… not even that there would be a tomorrow.

And Noah was a man who would protect her with his life—had already saved her once—and she couldn't possibly ask for anything better than that. *Anyone* better than that.

When she got to his apartment, she would show him exactly how grateful she was.

CHAPTER 9

The pounding in Noah's head from whacking it against the motel bathroom wall had subsided—but he was still kicking himself for putting Emily in that room in the first place. He quickly drove to his apartment, which wasn't far, then ushered her out of his car and up the elevator to his apartment. She'd been quiet the whole time, obviously still in shock, and he wanted to get her someplace he knew would be safe. He could have taken her to her own home, but honestly, he wanted to stay with her for a while, make sure her shock wasn't going into overdrive, and it would have been hard to come up with an excuse to stay in her apartment. At his place, he could keep her until he was sure she was okay… and then take her home.

Although it was already late. He should probably just tuck her into his bed and crash on the couch. But first, he wanted to make sure she was actually okay.

Noah flipped on the lights and held the door for her. Emily eased past him, flitting looks like she wasn't quite sure what was going on. He closed the door behind them and ushered her toward the living room. He'd only been stateside a couple months, and he'd just moved in a few weeks ago—he hadn't had much to unpack, and even less in the way of décor, so the place screamed *bachelor living*. But it was clean. And the couch was comfortable enough.

"Please, sit down," he said, gesturing to the brown faux-suede couch.

She perched on the edge, looking nervous.

He knelt next to her, getting a good look at her face. The tears had dried, thank God. That had about undone him. And she seemed calm if still a little wide-eyed. "Are you too warm or too cold? Sometimes shock can chill you."

She smiled, tentatively. "No, I'm good. I think… yeah, I was definitely in shock there for a while. My head was buzzing." She gave him a sheepish look.

"But you're feeling better now?" he asked. That was a really good sign, actually. That she'd already had some symptoms, but they had passed.

"Yeah." The smile was back, stronger.

"How about something to eat? Or drink? I don't have much, but—"

"Just come sit with me, Noah." She patted the couch next to her.

"Yeah. Okay." That surprised him, but he was quickly by her side, knee-to-knee on the couch. He couldn't resist tucking a wayward piece of her long, blonde hair behind her ear. "Please tell me you're really okay."

"You've asked me, like, fifteen times." She smirked a little. "This is as okay as I get."

He smiled, and the relief was real. She sounded like herself again. He bit his lip. "Just feeling guilty, I guess."

She leaned toward him, touching his cheek, suddenly close.

All the breath went out of his body.

"You don't need to feel guilty," she said softly. "I wasn't doing anything I didn't want to do."

Then she shocked the hell out of him by leaning in further and kissing him. It was just a soft brush of her lips on his, and then she was pulling back, watching his reaction... but it lit a fire in him that reflexively had him reaching for her, bringing her back for more. She moved closer on the couch, digging her hands into his hair and deepening the kiss.

He held back the moan and forced himself to pull back. "Emily," he whispered, his voice hoarse. "Are you sure about this? You've just been through—"

"I almost died." Her voice was a whisper, but it froze him. Then she kissed him again, just that soft touch, and pulled back to look into his eyes. "You saved my life. And I want to live it."

Oh, man... he was in such trouble with this. "Are you sure?"

She didn't answer, just pressed her soft lips to his.

His beast was growling with need, and he wasn't at all sure this was wise, but he couldn't force himself to say no. He pulled her tighter into the kiss, then hooked his arm around her waist and eased her into his lap. She was so short, she fit perfectly—her tight bottom on his legs, pressing against his quickly growing erection, her lips at just the right level for kissing, and her body calling to his

ALISA WOODS

hands. He had one at the back of her head, bunched in her hair, angling her so he could plunder her mouth with his tongue. Her small moans, deep in her throat were driving him wild. He wanted to devour every inch of her sweetness. His other hand slid under her t-shirt, along her hot skin to the back, unhooking her bra, so he could have free rein with her breasts, which were pulling against the fabric of her shirt and taunting him as she arched her back.

His beast ached for her. Noah growled and nipped his way down her neck, taking small tastes as he went. Her gasps and heaving chest were ramping up his desire like crazy. He wanted, no *needed,* to hear her screaming his name. He shoved up her bra, his hand still under her shirt, and roughly grasped the fullness of her breast. The mewling sound that came out of her mouth and the insanely tight perking of her nipple on his palm just drove him on harder. He yanked up her shirt, eager to get his mouth on that sweet bud, but when he did, she gasped in a way that was *not good…* and pulled away.

She hastily pulled her shirt back down and folded in on herself with hunched shoulders.

"God, Em, did I… did I hurt you?" He hadn't even reached her breast with his mouth, but maybe, somehow, he had hurt some something along the way. She was so small and delicate…

"No. No." She was shaking her head, but it wasn't entirely for him. She stared down at the hem of her shirt, twisting it in her hands. "No," she said again, more resolutely, then smoothed down the shirt and looked up at him. "No, I want to do this."

He frowned. "We don't have to do this."

"No, I want to." She nodded, like she was convincing herself, then she scooted closer again, putting her arms around his neck and brushing his lips with hers.

But she was *shaking*.

He stopped her. "What's wrong?"

"Nothing, I just…" She swallowed. "I just… haven't done this in a while. Out of practice. That's all."

He held still, even more unsure now. His first thought at their original hookup was that she was far too nervous—that maybe this was her first time, not just with a WildLove hookup, but with sex of any kind. That thought came rushing back—if she simply didn't want to admit it before, for some odd reason… "Are you sure this isn't, you know, actually your first time doing this?" he asked as gently as he could.

She pulled back, suddenly cold, and he instantly

regretted the words. "Very sure." She wrapped her arms tight around her chest, locking him out completely.

God, he was an idiot. "Emily, it's really okay if it is. I didn't mean anything bad, I just—"

"It was my uncle."

Her words stopped him cold. His entire body froze while his mind sprinted to catch up. "Your *what?*"

She stared at the couch between them. "My uncle. Just once. I was sixteen." Her hands were turning white with how hard each finger was digging into her arms.

His skin was ice cold, a frozen sheet that barely contained the surging anger of his beast. His mouth struggled for words while his mind fought to keep his wolf inside, contained… because all of sudden, it wanted to *kill something.*

Her brow scrunched up, and she slowly dragged her gaze up to his. She was expecting him to say something—to *respond,* for fuck's sake—but he was still molten lava under the ice sheet, barely keeping himself together.

"Is he still alive?" Noah had to force the words out. They were rough. Abrasive.

She leaned back, like that was the last thing she expected him to say. "No. Car crash. Couple years ago."

The ice holding him together broke, but he didn't explode. Didn't shift. Instead, it was just enough release to keep him human.

"Good," he said, voice still rough. "Otherwise, I would have had to kill him."

Her eyes went wide.

He rubbed both hands over his face, still trying to come back from losing it altogether. He meant every word, and he would gladly have ripped that goddamn rapist uncle into small, bloody chunks, but he knew that wasn't what this was really about—her uncle wasn't the man Noah truly wanted to kill. That volcanic anger was years of wanting to kill the one man he never could… *his father.*

For doing exactly that to Noah's mother. Repeatedly. For years.

He swallowed down the sickness rising at the back of his throat—the memories flooded back, the barely suppressed knowledge that he had, as a child, known all along what was happening to his mother. Straight up until he found her bleeding out on the kitchen floor.

"I… I should probably go." Emily's whispery voice barely registered.

But when it did, it snapped him out of his haze.

"What?"

But she was already scrambling off the couch. "I understand," she said.

"Understand *what?*" He caught her around the waist, holding her from fleeing. She was trying to *leave*. Because he fucking handled this like a moron. An emotionally crippled moron.

"It's okay," she mumbled, pushing ineffectually at his hands holding her. "Most guys wouldn't want to... it's okay. I understand."

"No." He lurched up off the couch, looming over her, stopping her frantic attempts to run away, before he thought about what he was doing. She cringed under him, eyes flying wide and terrified. He immediately softened his hold on her waist, then let her go, and eased back, not touching her any longer. "Emily, please don't leave." He swallowed down his regret for not doing this better and poured every bit of non-verbal beseeching he could into his eyes. "Please stay. Let me explain."

The wildness in her eyes calmed, and a small puzzled look took over her face. "You don't have to explain. I know it's strange to find out that—"

"Please." He was flat-out begging her now. "I *do* have to explain. And then I want to kiss you again. And more.

If you'll let me." He had a small tremble of fear run through him—ice cold and terrifying and not something he'd felt in a long, long time—all because the uncertain look on her face made it seem like she might leave anyway.

"You still want to kiss me?" She said this like it was almost impossible for her to understand.

"God, yes." Then he reached for her, just for her hands, and gently brought them to his lips, kissing the backs. "And so much more. Please just… sit with me. Let me explain."

She seemed dazed but nodded. He eased back down to the couch, bringing her with him.

"I know you think wolves are, well, these amazingly good guys…" he started, but then stalled out at the shine in her eyes. He was going to crush her fantasy about shifters, but it couldn't be helped. He swallowed, and continued, "But not all wolves are good."

She just waited for him to go on, hands clasped in her lap.

"You may have heard about my father, Colonel Wilding."

"He was in charge of the experiments," she said softly. "Including the ones on you. I know."

He nodded. "Yeah, well, he wasn't exactly a stellar guy at home, either." Noah sucked in a breath and let it out slow. It had been so long since he'd really thought about this, and besides his sister, Piper, and his brother, Daniel, he hadn't really discussed it with *anyone*. It wasn't the kind of thing people wanted to hear. "My father basically kidnapped my mother and forced her to mate with him."

Emily's horrified look sent a twinge of shame through him.

He hurried through the rest. "That's not the way mating is supposed to work, but female wolves are in short supply, and some assholes don't want to miss out, so they basically steal what they would never be able to win over by choice. My father was that kind. He killed the man my mother was mated to, breaking the bond so he could take her as his own mate. And once the new mating bond took hold, there was no way for my mother to break free. It's a bond for life. And for years…" Noah fought through the closing up of his throat. "For years, my father used that against her. I grew up watching her slowly waste away under the daily abuse of being mated to a man she didn't love. For as long as I can remember, I knew the only reason me and my brother existed was because he *forced* himself upon her."

Noah didn't realize his fists were clenched, balled up on top of his knees until Emily's small, warm hand landed on one of them.

"Noah," she said, her voice full of pain, "I'm so sorry."

He forced himself to finish what he had to say. "My mother eventually killed herself. I was the first to find her bleeding out on the floor of our kitchen. I was eleven."

"Oh my God." Emily was up on her knees on the couch, throwing her arms around him again. The shaking was gone, from her at least, although now Noah felt like he could barely force his hands to unlock to hold her steady against the softness of the cushions. "I'm so, so sorry," she whispered.

"It's okay," he said, fighting back all the horror that day always conjured. He gently eased her back so he could look her in the eyes. "I wanted you to know so you would understand my reaction to… to this horrible thing your uncle did to you. And so you'd know that if there were any way I could fix that for you, I would. Men like that don't deserve to keep breathing." He lightly touched her cheek with just his fingertips. "You bring out the alpha in me, Em. The one that wants to protect you from anything bad in this world. Because you should be loved and cherished and never forced to do anything, least of all that. I can't do anything about your uncle now, but if you'll let me, I want to show you how a woman should be loved." He meant every word, even if those words surprised them as they came out of his mouth. Because it was *this* that had been drawing him to her all this time— her passion for wolves, her belief in the good side of them, and this vulnerability in her that his alpha sensed from the beginning. She had been *hurt…* and somehow his beast knew that Noah could be the one to help her heal.

Emily seemed to fight for words, but eventually, she said, "Maybe not all wolves are good. But Noah Wilding, you are everything I ever thought they might be."

He couldn't help but smile. She didn't know about his lineage, the white wolf and what that meant, but he would take it. He would let her believe he was good because it was what she needed, right here, right now.

"Good enough to kiss?" he asked, the smile growing a little.

"Good enough to be my first," she said, eyes shining. Then she climbed into his lap, legs to the side, hands weaving into his hair. "I believe this is where we left off," she said softly, then she pressed her lips to his.

He soaked in her gentle touch, then brushed her hair back from her face, taking her cheeks in his hands and kissing her softly in return. He felt her breath quicken, but he kept his pace slow and measured, teasing touches over her clothes, light strokes with his tongue, tender nibbles at her neck. Her hands were becoming more frantic on his shoulders and in his hair, and it had his cock straining against his pants, but he just eased her up to standing in front of him. He needed her clothes off in order to please her the way he wanted to. He lifted her shirt and gently kissed her sweet belly as he undid her jeans and slipped them down her legs. Her panties went next, and when she stepped out of them, he slid her delicious little bare bottom back into his lap.

With one hand held at her back, the other slid under her shirt to sweep caresses across her breasts. Her nipples were hard again, and it took everything he had not to tug her shirt off and feast upon them. But her reaction before meant he had to go slow… and he would go as slow as it took to get her there. The pink rising in her cheeks, the nearly soundless heaving of her chest, the aching parting of her lips… all of it was giving him the hard-on of his life. But there was no way he was doing anything but *gentle* for her in this first time she was with a man voluntarily. It was a gift of trust she was giving him, and he wanted to pay it back with an orgasm she would never forget.

She was tugging at his shirt. "Noah!" It was a cry of frustration.

"Would you like this off?" he asked, his own breath ragged.

"Yes!"

He reached back to pull his shirt off over his head, having to release her for a moment to get it free. Then her hands were roaming his chest and his shoulders, her hot breath on his cheek as her delicate fingers were setting his skin on fire.

"You like that?" he breathed into her ear as he nuzzled her cheek.

"Oh God, yes." Her lips traveled down his neck, nibbling at his shoulders with little kitten bites that were making him moan.

He slid his hand under her shirt again, playing with her nipple, then cupping her breast, and gently kneading it. "How about this?"

"Yes. *More.*"

"Yes, Ma'am." His hand trailed down her belly and slipped between her legs.

She gasped, but it was the good kind. Still, he asked, "Are you all right?"

"Yes." She eased her legs apart, giving him greater access. The scent of her arousal was like a cloud around her, a perfume of desire that was making his head swim. When he lightly slid his fingers along her sex, he found she was already *so* wet for him.

"You're making me crazy," he whispered into her neck between kisses.

She whimpered as his fingers slid across her sex a little faster. He lightly touched her most sensitive nub, and she shuddered so deliciously in his arms that he wasn't sure he was going to be able to keep up this slow pace. She grabbed his face in her delicate hands and kissed him deeply. He probed her mouth with his tongue as he slipped a finger slowly inside her. She tensed just for a second, then kissed him even more furiously.

His cock was straining so hard against his jeans he was afraid it might burst out.

Her hands found his chest again, grabbing at him, pulling him closer even though he was already inside her, slowly thrusting, even if it was just with his finger—first one, and then two. She moaned when he slipped in the second, then made that kitten-mewling sound again as he brushed her nub with his thumb. God, the sounds she was making.

"Ms. Emily Jones," he said hoarsely, "I need your shirt off, my love. Is that all right?"

She instantly released her clawing hold on him and quickly dragged off her t-shirt and the hapless bra left hanging from before. His hand was still working her, thrusting slowly inside, in and out, and she was panting all through it. Once her clothes were on the floor, he eased her back on the couch, holding himself above her, still pleasuring her with his hand. Her head tipped, her back arched, and her nipples pointed in the air, calling to his tongue. Her pale skin was everywhere flushed with the pleasure he was giving her, and he'd never seen anything so beautiful in his life.

He eased himself down, his hand still between her legs, his chest brushing against hers, rocking with her as he felt her pleasure gain speed.

"Goddamn, you are so beautiful, Em." His breath was ragged on her face, his own need for her aching deep inside him. "I want you so badly."

Her hands gripped his shoulders, and her head lifted. "Make love to me, Noah."

He grinned. "I am, my love." He thrust a little harder

with his hand for emphasis.

She dropped her head back and groaned. "I want you inside me!"

He rocked his body harder against her, plunging deeper with his hand. She arched up against him and gasped.

He nuzzled her cheek. "I *am* inside you, Em. Come for me, and I'll do anything you ask." Then he worked his way down her neck, soft kisses that grew stronger, turning to wet bites that devoured her sweet skin until he reached the luscious mounds of her breasts. He took her nipple in his mouth, his moan mixing with hers. She was grabbing at him now, crying out sounds of pleasure. He swore he might come just listening to her. She bucked and cried out and suddenly her sweet flesh was convulsing around his hand, his fingers working the pleasure from her body in gasps and moans and quivering wetness. He kept going until she sunk into the couch, all tension released and skin glowing. A very masculine pride welled up in him: *he had pleasured her.* And by the looks of it, it was an orgasm she'd remember.

Her soft hands sought him, bringing his face back up to hers, but her eyes were still shut. She kissed him and said, "Oh, my God, Noah."

"I'll take that as a compliment." He couldn't help the grin.

She finally opened her eyes. "Is it always like that?"

"No." He grinned wider. "It definitely gets better."

Her eyes went wide. "I'm not sure I can survive better."

He kissed her, eased his hand slowly from between her legs, then kissed her quickly again on the nose. "I certainly hope you can. Because I am far from done with you, Ms. Jones."

He loved her look of hunger—of just flat-out lust in her eyes—as he stood and unbuttoned his pants.

CHAPTER 10

Emily stared at Noah as he slid off his jeans and his cock sprung free.

There was beautiful male anatomy—gorgeously sculpted muscles, thick pulsing cocks—and then there was *Noah*. Mouth-wateringly taut stomach, strong thighs that looked like they could bench press her Prius, and a cock so long and thick and stiff that she seriously doubted it could fit inside her. She couldn't wait to touch him, so she did—she swung her legs off the couch, slid her hand along his satin-skinned cock and wrapped her lips around it.

"Holy—" Noah pulled back before she could even get a good taste. "Oh no," he said with a dangerous smile. "None of that. Not yet, at least. God, Em, I'll never make it through if you do that."

"What then?" she asked, licking her lips. "You said you'd do anything I asked." The orgasm she'd just come down from—that Noah had given her with only his fingers and his mouth—had loosened something inside her. Made her bold and hungry for more. She was with him, in this moment, and she was going to have every inch of it… and him.

His grin was back. "I did say that, didn't I?" But instead of answering her, he sat on the couch next to her and pulled her toward him. "But first things first. Straddle me, Em."

Her eyes went wide, and as her gaze dropped to his cock, now standing tall up from where he sat, she wondered again if it really could fit. It seemed doubtful. And something else occurred to her that she hadn't even thought of before, in the heat of wanting him.

"Shouldn't we have, you know, protection?" she asked.

He eased her into his lap, facing him this time, but she wasn't quite lined up to take his enormous, gorgeous cock inside her. Yet.

He smiled as he caressed her breast and rolled her nipple between his fingers. "Want to know something about wolves that few humans do, Ms. Emily Jones?"

She leaned into his touch, bringing her arms up to wrap around his neck. "Always."

"We can scent a woman's fertility. Wolf or human." He slipped his hand down her belly to between her legs again, sending an insanely delicious rush of pleasure through her.

She couldn't imagine how much better it would be with him inside. "What does that mean?" she asked, breathlessly, although she was caring less by the second.

"It means I know I can make love to you ten times tonight and not make any babies." He gently thrusted two fingers inside her, making her squirm. But she didn't want his hand.

"Are you sure?" she panted against his cheek.

"Very. I'm not the kind of wolf who spreads his seed around the human population, not carrying if his hookup is fertile, leaving his halflings to fend for themselves in his wake." He gently eased his hand out of her and held her back to look in her eyes. "If I make a baby with you, Emily Jones, it will be because we both want it."

His words and his touch and her need for him were all making her ache. Then he moved under her, sliding just a little so that his cock was lined up with her entrance. His hands on her hips were urging her to lower herself down, impale herself on him, and she didn't need any more encouragement. She felt his tip slip inside her, stretch her, already so much larger than his fingers had been.

She gasped and stopped. "You're so big," she breathed.

"Take as much time as you need," he said, but his voice was strained.

She lifted her hips a little then took him deeper. It felt like he was filling her completely, stretching her impossibly wide, but she hadn't even taken half of him inside yet. "Oh, God, Noah."

"Easy," he said, voice rough. He lifted his hips, pressing a little deeper, then pulling back again. "You're so tight, Em. God, you feel good."

The fact that she was pleasuring him drove her on. She took a breath, forced her body to relax, leaned in to kiss him… and sank down fully on his cock.

"Holy fuck," he whispered against her lips, then his

head tipped back on the couch. "You're killing me, Em," he said to the ceiling. "I might die in the process of loving you, but it's so going to be worth it."

She grinned and slipped her hand behind his neck, lifting his head back up to look at her. "Don't die yet. I'm not done with you."

"God, woman," he breathed. "Please move."

Already her body had adjusted to the massive fullness of having him inside her... so she did. Lifting her hips then pressing back down, just once, wrenched a moan out of both of them. She did it again, and again, each time getting a little easier as the wetness gushed between her legs.

"Oh Jesus," Noah whispered. "So tight. So good. Ride me, Em. Harder."

She couldn't even form words. The pleasure was insane and building fast. Each stroke was a lightning rod straight to the hot nerves in her sex, stretching wide all around him, hugging him tight, taking him deeper inside with each stroke. His hands held her body, warm and firm, guiding her and urging her on. Then he slid one to the front, circling her still-sensitive nub with his thumb. She shrieked with the bolt of pleasure that shot through her, tipping her head back, gripping his shoulders, and pounding down on him as hard as she could. Stars swam in front of her eyes as the pleasure rushed to a peak then exploded throughout her body, pulsing from where she and Noah were connected, joining bodies and moans in one cascade of sound and pleasure. It was so much *more* than the first time. As the waves of her orgasm started to subside, she slowed her pace, but kept riding him, kept moving, kept taking him deep inside.

He was still hard. Just as hard and full as before. Right as she was wondering if she'd done something wrong, Noah's strained voice broke through the haze of pleasure buzzing her brain.

"Emily," he gasped.

"Yes?" She looked down at his face, hardened with something that might be pain, but she didn't think it was.

"I want to take you like this," he said, voice rough. He held her tight as he shifted positions, laying her back on the couch with him on top. His cock was still buried inside her, connecting them with something indescribably intimate as he peered into her eyes.

"You're the most beautiful thing in this world, Emily Jones," he said, voice still tight, but more under control. "Tell me I can have you this way." He slid almost all the way out and then thrust back in, harder than any thrust she had been able to manage perched on top of him.

She let out a breath of surprise then reached for him, digging her hands into his back. "Harder," she said, looking straight into his eyes.

He groaned, his eyes hooding with pleasure, then he thrust into her again. Still fresh off her last orgasm, she didn't think she could feel any more pleasure, but *this*... this was something entirely new. He thrust again and again, each time jolting fresh heights of pleasure through her.

His groan turned into a growl. "You are *mine*. All mine." Each thrust was another possessive pulse, pushing her higher. Then something deep inside her wound tighter than it had ever been and released in an orgasm so hard it had her throwing her head back, screaming his name, and bucking so hard against him that she lifted them both momentarily off the couch. Noah's growl went guttural, and he froze. She could feel his release, pulsing hot, filling her with that seed that he promised wouldn't make babies for her.

Even as she fell through the cascade of her receding waves of pleasure, she believed him in his promise... and almost wished it weren't true. Because she could already feel the heartbreak, the separation that would come, first their bodies, and then more. It would have to come eventually because Noah Wilding was a shifter, and a shifter wouldn't keep a human like her. She wished for a small piece of him to take with her… a child with his warm smile and gentle eyes. It was utterly foolish to wish for such a thing, but she let herself do it, just for a moment, while he was still inside her, still groaning his release, still coming down from the peak of pleasure he'd driven her to three times. And when he finally pulled out, lifting himself away from her, disconnecting, she let that little dream die… as it should.

She wouldn't regret any of this, no matter if it was all there would ever be.

Because she had never felt more fully alive in her life as she did in that moment… and she owed it all to Noah Wilding.

Noah nestled his face into the crook of her neck, still breathing hard. "I think I might have died and gone to heaven." His arm was heavy across her chest, even though he was holding most of his weight off her, but the thick post-pleasure haze enveloped them both like a cocoon, and Emily wouldn't move out of it for anything.

They lay that way until their breathing calmed.

Then Noah lifted his head to look in her eyes. "You

okay?" he asked gently.

"Much better than okay." She smiled.

He returned her smile, and it lit her from within. Then he kissed her softly on the lips and rose up from the couch. A small pain sliced through her chest. Was it already over? Would he send her home? But before she could get too far with that train of thought, much less make it off the couch, Noah scooped her up into his arms. He was ridiculously strong, as if lifting her and cradling her to his chest took no effort at all.

Then suddenly they were moving. "Where are we going?" she asked, although it quickly became apparent they were heading toward the back of his apartment.

"I'd love to say I'm taking you to bed for more sex," he said with a smirk, "but you need to rest." He kicked open the bedroom door, crossed the room, and carefully laid her on the bed.

For a moment, she was afraid he might leave her there, alone, but then he climbed over her, tugging back the blankets and rearranging the pillows. It wasn't a large bed—really meant for one—but he tucked her into his chest, spooning her from behind as he pulled the blankets up to cover her quickly-cooling skin. It was all so gentle and thoughtful and sweet, it pricked tears to her eyes. She was glad she was turned away from him so he wouldn't see.

"Are you comfortable?" he asked.

She murmured her yes, and his hands found a home on her body, carefully holding her like she was something breakable and precious. A tear slowly slid down her cheek; she didn't brush it away, for fear of letting him know it was there.

"Rest, sweet Emily," he whispered in her ear.

So she closed her eyes and did.

CHAPTER 11

Noah noticed something was missing even before he opened his eyes.

Emily.

His eyes popped open as his hands found the cold sheets next to him. He stilled, listening for her in the bathroom or outside his bedroom in the apartment... *nothing.*

Had she left already? He was surprised how much that thought instantly chilled him, almost as much as the empty space her small body had occupied in his bed.

Maybe she was just being quiet. He practically launched himself out of the bed, searching the bathroom and kitchen and living room, but his apartment just wasn't that big. And Emily definitely wasn't in it.

The chill in his chest trickled into his stomach and made it clench. Her words from before, when they first met, hurtled back to him: *I just wanted one night. That's all.* That was all it was supposed to be from the beginning. And he understood why, now that she'd told him what had happened with her uncle. Maybe she'd gotten what she wanted from Noah—a hot night of sex—and now she was gone.

He shook his head as if to fling that thought away. That didn't make sense, not the way they were together last night. They hadn't simply fucked… they'd made love. He knew the difference—but maybe she didn't. Maybe this crazy feeling he had that he was falling in love with her… maybe that was just *him*. Or worse—maybe last night had triggered some kind of flashback and she'd fled.

His heart sank with that thought.

He was still naked from their lovemaking, but when he scrambled to find his pants, it wasn't because he was bothering with clothes—he wanted his phone. Just as he found her number in his recent calls, he saw there was a message from her.

Took a taxi back to the office. New idea re:tracking bad guys. Call you soon.

His pounding heart settled a little as he read her text, but it still left him feeling empty. Back to the office. Back to the bad guys. No mention of the time they'd spent together.

Noah rubbed his face with his free hand. Was he really this wrapped up in this girl? Couldn't he just be casual about it, the way she was? But the tight knot in his stomach answered that for him: *no.* It hadn't really been casual for him from that first moment she stepped through the motel door all trembling and brave, trying to do something to change her life. To heal herself from wounds he didn't even know she had. Not from the minute she softly petted his wolf form or declared she would catch the bad guys targeting shifters even though she was human herself.

No, it had all been a fast downhill slide into loving Emily Jones after that.

And it wasn't "WildLove"—a fast hookup—but the real kind.

He wasn't about to screw that up or let her slip away.

Noah texted quickly. *Missed you when I woke up. Call me.* Then he grabbed his clothes and headed for the shower. While the water washed away all traces of their lovemaking from the night before, he thought through what this hard-ache feeling inside him truly meant.

He was a white wolf—whatever that truly was—and he was falling in love with a human.

He knew what his brother, Daniel, would say about that—forget her and move on. But Daniel didn't know what Noah was... and in some ways, he didn't really know, either. What it meant or what he was capable of. By the time he finished his shower, he had hoped Emily would have called or at least texted back: *nothing.* While he was waiting for that to happen, he needed to get his head straight about who he was and what he was doing with her... before he got in any deeper.

And for that, he knew just who he needed to talk to: *Owen Harding.*

Owen was mated to Noah's cousin, Nova Wilding, but more importantly, he'd been transformed into a white wolf by the experiments, just like Noah. Only Noah was pretty sure Owen wasn't a secret male witch as well. Maybe. That was a conversation he was overdue in having, especially given the Texan was older than Noah, mated now, and probably considering pups as well. In short, he might be able to help Noah sort out this mess that he was.

Noah sent a quick text to his brother, Daniel, saying he wouldn't be returning to the safehouse this morning—it appeared they had no more leads on the bomber from last night anyway—then he texted Owen to see if he could swing by Wylderide. Owen had given up his job with Riverwise security to be alpha of the pack there, as well as help run the company, so it was a good bet he was in the office this morning.

Bingo. *Sure*, Owen texted back. *Always got time for ya'll.*

Be there in twenty, Noah replied, then grabbed his keys and headed out.

A quick drive across town, and Noah was cruising into the Wylderide office on the twenty-fourth floor of a gleaming high-rise in downtown Seattle. He gathered a few nods on the way in—Noah had helped rescue their CEO, so the pack was pretty friendly to Riverwise these days—but he didn't stop, heading straight to Owen's office. It was empty, so he swung into Nova's next door.

Nova and Owen were both at her desk, gathered around her screen, holding hands while they discussed something. They were pretty damn cute together. You could practically see the mating bond between them, something that Noah would never have, not fully, no matter what he decided to do with Emily.

Nova noticed him first. "Hey, cuz!" she said brightly, waving him in.

"Where's the fire?" Owen asked with that Southern drawl he has. "You sure got here fast."

"Can I borrow your mate for a few minutes?" he asked Nova. To Owen, he said, "It's not an emergency or anything." Although his bunched-up stomach wanted to disagree with that.

Owen frowned but rose up from his chair. "Nova just barely tolerates me poking into the business anyway."

"That's not true!" she protested.

"True enough that you can spare me for a bit." Owen gave her a small smile.

"Well, all right," Nova said, making a show of shooing him out. "But only because it's Noah. And get back here when you're done! I want to finalize these game specs before we let the designers loose on them."

"Hold on… who's alpha around here, again?" Owen said with a smirk, but he was already at the door with Noah.

Nova mock-scowled at him. "You're alpha when I say

you are."

"Guess I'll have to come back and prove you wrong." Owen's smirk was loaded with all kinds of promises Noah really didn't need to see.

Nova's eyes flashed in return.

"Come on, guys," Noah complained. "Give a bachelor wolf a break. I do *not* need to know what you're doing in this office when the door's closed."

Owen just chuckled and clapped a hand on Noah's shoulder, ushering him out of the room. Once they were inside Owen's office with the door closed behind them, the older wolf's face grew more serious. "I hear you guys are having it rough with the WildLove bomber," he said. "Glad to see you're in one piece."

"White wolves are hard to kill," Noah said, jumping right into it.

Owen's eyebrows lifted. "Is that right?"

Noah nodded. Owen had to know his own white wolf had amazing healing properties—Noah had witnessed it first hand when Owen had come back practically from the dead.

"So this is about the experiments, then," Owen said gravely. "Did they give you the freakish claws as well?"

Noah shifted just his hands and let his claws come

out, revealing the foot-long knives that he knew Owen possessed as well.

Owen whistled. "Between that and the extreme healing, it almost makes the year I was in the cages worthwhile." He folded his arms and leaned back against his desk.

"Yeah, well, I'd still prefer it hadn't happened." Noah grimaced. "Plus, there's more. At least, there's more to this for me. I think. That's what I came to ask you about. Have you had any other... *abilities*... that came with being a white wolf?"

Owen's eyes narrowed. "How do you mean?"

"Any magical abilities that maybe go beyond the standard blood magic for shifters?" Noah swallowed. He'd never told anyone about this part. About what he could *do*.

"Can't say as I have," Owen said carefully. "Although I haven't exactly pushed it, if you know what I mean."

"I do." Noah had spent considerable time getting his beast under control after he was released from the cages. He watched Owen go through it as well. And it wasn't like Noah was *eager* to push his white wolf to its limits... it had just sort of happened. "But you aren't the only white wolf I know."

Owen frowned. "Well, there's Grace Krepky."

Noah nodded. She was mated to Jared River, one of the three brothers who ran Riverwise. These days, she was running for Congress, one of the events that had tipped the hate group into high gear and had them targeting the Wilding and River packs, and now expanding their sights even further to other wolves through WildLove.

"But apparently Grace has been a white wolf all her life," Noah said. "I hear she has the rapid healing, but not the claws. Then there's you and me, turned into white wolves by the experiments with the complete set— healing and claws both. But there's someone else. Someone in my family."

"Daniel?" Owen asked, both eyebrows hiked up again.

"Not as far as I know." Then again, Noah hadn't told his brother about *his* white wolf, either, so maybe they both had secrets. "But maybe. Turns out the secret Wilding family shame is that one of our grandfathers was a white wolf."

"Shame?" Owen gave him a skeptical look. "Doesn't seem like the kind of thing to be ashamed of, necessarily."

"Well, that's the thing." Noah gritted his teeth but just

forced it out. "Turns out my white wolf grandfather wasn't really a wolf at all. More of a male witch."

Owen straightened and unfolded his arms. "You don't say."

"Yeah, and now…" Noah grimaced.

"Now you think you're following in the old man's steps." Owen rubbed his face. "Shit, Noah, how does that even work?"

Noah lifted his hands. "I don't know. That's the problem."

Owen scowled. "You never did tell me what happened in Afghanistan. And I'm not buying that story about your medical discharge being for PTSD. I've seen grunts that have it. You don't."

Noah shook his head. "No, I just convinced the psych staff that I needed out. Considering the experiments, they didn't argue."

"So, what really brought you back home?"

"I just couldn't take the risk of being there anymore." Noah took a breath and rushed out the story. "I was on patrol, clearing out bad guys from a part of the city that'd already taken artillery. Going door-to-door. It was completely emptied out, but you know, we have to make sure. So we split up to cover more ground, and I was on my own when I stumbled on a pack of them. Five altogether. They jumped me, shot the hell out of me, and if it weren't for the superhealing, that would have been it. Instead… I killed every last one of them."

Owen was listening to him intently. "So you fought back when you should have been dead. That doesn't make you a witch, Noah."

"No, but turning them all into piles of ash does."

Owen's eyes went wide. "Well… that's something."

"Yeah. The strange thing is that I didn't even touch them. I just somehow *felt* where they were and… lashed out."

"Could you do it again?" Owen was looking at him with a mix of horror and fascination.

"Haven't exactly wanted to try." Noah rubbed both hands on his temples. "Look, I can't tell anyone about this. I mean, I *was* a wolf, for fuck's sake. I grew up a wolf. Even now, my beast form is definitely a white wolf. I just… have these other abilities…"

"But they only showed up after the cages?" Owen asked.

"All of it was after the experiments. They triggered something inside me. That's why I was wondering if you've had anything happen, anything that might make you suspect…"

But Owen was already shaking his head. "No, nothing like that. My white wolf is powerful, don't get me wrong, but he's all wolf." He peered at Noah. "Sounds like you're some kind of hybrid—witch and wolf—although I'll be damned if I even know what that means."

Noah nodded, shoulders dropping. He was afraid that's exactly what it was.

"I'm no fan of witches in general, but there are a few good ones out there," Owen said quietly. "This doesn't have to be something you're ashamed of. You are who you are, Noah. And from where I stand, what you are is a wolf I'd have at my back any day of the week."

Noah gave him a wry smile. "Thanks. But it's more complicated than that. There's this girl, Emily…"

Owen smirked. "They do tend to complicate things."

"Yeah, well, this one isn't even a wolf." Noah sighed. "And I think I'm falling for her."

The smile fled from Owen's face. "Well, that's a different story."

"She loves wolves. She thinks *I'm* a wolf. Which I *am*." Noah sighed. "Who am I kidding? I don't know what the hell I am."

Owen eased away from the desk and took a couple

steps toward him. "Look, you helped me see my way straight to fighting for Nova," he said, his hand landing on Noah's shoulder. "So I'm going to return the favor. If this girl is the one, don't let the fact that she's human and you're… whatever you are… stop you. If I've learned one thing about finding the mate you're supposed to be with, it's that it's rarely convenient. But it's always worth the trouble. *Always.*"

Noah frowned. Those were the words he wanted to hear, but at the same time, this was a completely unknown thing. It would have been complicated enough, if he were a merely wolf—the mating would be one-sided, but at least it had been done before. This thing of crossing a half-wolf-half-witch-whatever-the-hell-he-was with a human?

"What about pups? Or kids?" Noah asked. "I'm not even sure what to call them."

Owen smiled. "Cross that road when you get there, my friend."

Noah swallowed. "Right." He pulled his phone from his pocket. Still no text from Emily. "Look, I should let you get back to your mate for whatever sex date you have planned for her office."

Owen's smile grew into a smirk. "And you need to go

after that girl—the one you don't think will have you."

Noah gave a small huff of a laugh, but Owen was dead-on. Emily loved wolves, but what would she think if she knew the truth about him?

All he knew was that he was already missing her like a piece of him had marched out of his body and walked away. But he could play it cool, just check in on her at her office, see where she was with this whole thing between them last night. Maybe she was just looking for a one-night thing. Maybe that's all she needed from him to heal her past.

He'd simply be cool about it and find out.

Right.

He hurried so fast to the elevator, he almost forgot to wave goodbye to Owen.

CHAPTER 12

Emily drummed her nails on the counter as she waited for the Keurig to brew her coffee.

She'd cleared out early and left Noah sleeping, curled up cutely in his bed. Eyes closed, face peaceful. Shock of brown hair all mussed from their lovemaking. It had been hard to wrench herself out of his warm embrace, much less manage to sneak out without waking him, but it was better this way. Easier for him to make the clean break she knew was coming. One-time, no attachments. Back to work like it hadn't happened. It would be easier for both of them.

At least, that's what she kept telling herself all the way in to the office.

She'd sent a text so he wouldn't worry. Not that he would worry. Not that he would wake up with the pleasantly-sore feeling she had between her legs with every small movement of her body that reminded her of the passion-filled night they'd shared. No, he would probably just wake up, see the text, and go about his day. Maybe head back to Riverwise. Possibly call her later. Only she said she'd call him. But it was too soon, so she couldn't. He wasn't up yet. But she wanted to. Just to hear his voice.

God, she was a mess with this.

The Keurig finally finished spitting out her coffee, so she grabbed her *Coffee Is My Boyfriend* mug and inhaled the steam like it was the answer to all her problems. The irony wasn't lost on her that she'd run away from the amazing man she'd slept with—both literally and figuratively—only to return to her normal routine where coffee was the most stimulating thing in her life.

I'm not running away, she told herself. *I'm giving Noah room to leave.*

As she strode back to her desk, the ache between her legs wasn't buying any of that bullshit. Her body had barely been able to handle Noah's expert lovemaking, but it was already ready for more, soreness notwithstanding. And her heart already had a Noah-shaped hole in it. It was only her mind that knew running back to Noah Wilding's bed would be nothing but heartbreak for all of them.

She would always treasure the night they had together... and she would just have to stuff the part of her that wanted more than one night in a drawer somewhere and throw away the key.

Emily plopped down into her chair and studied her screen. She hadn't even managed to log in yet. It was ridiculously early, so no one else was in. No one to catch her sobbing at her desk, if it came to that. She set down her mug, shoved her keyboard to the side, and laid her head down on her folded arms. How could she actually focus on work when her head was still filled with thoughts of Noah?

"Hard night?" a male voice asked.

She jumped clean into the air, literally falling out of her seat. A gasp of air leaped out of her, and she barely caught herself on the edge of the desk to keep from going down completely. As she struggled back into her chair, which was sliding around on the wheels, she managed to look up and see who had startled her so badly.

It was one of the cleaning staff. The building owners had a service that came in off-hours. The guy was a medium-sized man, older than her twenty-one years— maybe thirty?—and he was grinning at her as if catching office workers in the dead of morning was some kind of prank he liked to play.

"You scared the crap out of me…" She peered at his name tag. "…Richard." She'd never seen him before. Usually the cleaning staff was comprised of short Polish women, but that was the night-time crew. She was never in this early.

"Sorry, Ms. Jones," he said with a smirk that brought wrinkles to the corners of his eyes. He didn't look sorry at all. "Thought you might need some help." His eyes were dark, and they flicked a look at her screen. "You all right here?"

"Yes, I'm fine, thank you," she said. "Except for that small heart attack just now."

His eyes sparkled. "Come in early to work, did you?"

"I've got some things to catch up on." Awfully nosy

for the maintenance staff. She wondered briefly where his equipment was... no vacuum or other supplies were immediately obvious.

"Well, I won't keep you from it." He gave her a long look—too long, like he was looking for something, then he turned away and shuffled down the cubicle row.

Strange.

Emily grabbed her mug, took a sip, then set it down again. She had to get her head in the game. The bomber had escaped last night, and he was obviously on to them now. They needed some kind of strategy to flush him out again... a way to trap him that he wouldn't expect...

She logged in and brought up the WildLove database, poking around the archives of her message chats with Noah. But that just made her heart ache, along with the sweet ache of her body, and totally messed up her head again. She sighed, closed out the chat, and pulled up another part of the code for WildLove. There had to be some way to track this guy down. Riverwise would run his description and maybe the plates from the car, if they had them, and that might ferret the guy out. But Emily had his digital signature in here, somehow, if she could just suss it from the data. She'd captured the real-time feeds during their secure chat. That was where she should start. Somehow he'd gotten in—Emily would just have to keep at it until she figured out how.

She dove in, tapping at her keyboard, bringing up screen after screen of code and data. She was so immersed in what she was doing, she didn't hear the maintenance guy until he was nearly at the open door of her cubicle again. His heavy boots gave him away just as he arrived, swishing rough along the office's trim carpet. She looked up from her keyboard right as he swung into her cubicle, holding the wall with one hand and a dusting rag with the other. He must have been cleaning something because he had gloves on now.

"Hey, I had another question for you, Emily." His dark eyes bored into hers.

"What's that?" Her internal alarm system was ringing bells all of a sudden. *Emily?* How did he know her name? Oh right… it was on her cubicle wall.

He stepped into her cubicle and came way too close, leaning on her desk and peering at her screen.

"Um… trying to work here…" she said, leaning away from him in her chair. What was this guy's deal?

He turned and smiled wide. "I can see that."

What the—? "Look, I can call security if you'd like—" Her heart was suddenly pounding.

"But you haven't answered my question, Emily."

Holy shit, who was this crazy person? "What question?" She scooted her chair back, but there was nowhere to go—she was right up against the cubicle wall.

His eyes took on a crazy glint. "Why do you refuse to die?"

What? She tried to get out of her chair, run, scream— do *something*—but he just shoved her back into it.

"Keep quiet, and I won't have to hurt you," he sneered, but he wasn't looking at her. He kept flicking his eyes at her screen, and with a dawning horror, she realized... she was still logged into the WildLove database.

He was one of them—the hackers.

She lunged for the keyboard. He snarled and shoved her away, slamming her back into her chair—she hit so hard, she bounced and ended up on the floor as the chair rolled out from under her. Out of the corner of her eye, she saw him draw something black from the back of his pants. *She had no time.* She turned away like she was crawling under the desk to get away from him, but in reality, she was going for the power cords. She only needed a second... *there.* She yanked the cable from the wall, powering down her entire workstation.

"What the—" The man slammed on the keyboard, and the table jumped above her head. Coffee splashed off the side, a brown waterfall that doused the carpet in chai latte. "Fuck!"

Emily curled up against the wall, tucking her legs in and getting as far from him as she could. He crouched down to glare at her, and it was now very, very obvious that what he'd pulled from the back of his pants was a gun.

Because it was pointing straight at her face.

"Come on out of there," he growled.

She shook her head, although it was jittery. She was shaking all over. But the fact that he was down there with her, trying to get her to come out, meant she succeeded in cutting off his access to WildLove. She didn't know exactly who he was or why he was here, but it could really only be one thing... the bombers had given up on hacking the message system and come directly to the source.

"I said, come out!" His shout rang out across the office, but it was empty. No one was coming to rescue her. No one even knew this guy was here.

"No." Her defiance was a whisper, but it turned his face red.

174

He shook the tip of the gun at her, like it was a finger he was wagging. "Come out or I'll shoot you."

"You can't shoot me," she said, in awe of the words coming out of her mouth.

"Oh, yeah?" He pointed the gun at her foot, which was poking out from her tucked-up legs just enough to be shot.

"Wait, wait!" she yelled, hands out. "If you shoot, people will come."

The red in his face darkened. He glowered at her for a moment, then he rocked back on his heels and tucked the gun back into his pants.

She tried to calm her breathing, but her heart was racing like crazy, and air was chuffing in and out of her lungs like she was running a mile. Then suddenly he was crawling in after her and grabbing her foot.

"No!" she yelled, kicking at him and clawing at the fabric of the cubicle wall, the steel legs of her desk, anything to stop him, but none of it was any use. He was too strong—he hauled her out by her ankle, then a rough hand grabbed hold of her arm and yanked her up from the floor. Once she was upright, he held her by both arms with her rear end pressed painfully against the table. His wiry body in the maintenance uniform loomed over her—even though he wasn't much taller than she was, his muscular hands held her in an iron grip.

His breath was sour on her face, but that didn't turn her stomach as much as his ugly smile. "I didn't expect to find anyone in the office this morning," he growled in her face. "I didn't expect to find *you* at all, not after last night. When I saw you from our motel window, it took me a while to figure out where I knew you from. I told Shirley it couldn't be you, but she insisted. Said she'd seen you in the company reports, on the website and in the press. I thought for sure we would have blown you and that shifter into tiny bits, but then the news reports said there were no casualties."

Emily's heart sank further with every word.

He'd been there last night. He'd already tried to kill her once. He would certainly do it again.

She didn't say anything.

"I figured I'd have to hack into the server myself," he went on. "Shouldn't be as difficult from a computer inside the building. Didn't plan on having the lead programmer here to give me the password. Guess it's my lucky day."

He was going to kill her anyway—he was the kind of man who would, and he'd already tried once. But she'd be damned if she would give him access to an entire database of shifters to target next.

"I'm not giving you access to *anything.*" She glared up into his face.

He chuckled darkly, and his hands tightened painfully on her arms. "We'll see about that."

Then her phone chimed from where it sat on the desk next to her mouse. They both looked. Emily's heart sank even further as she saw the popup: *Noah Wilding.*

Missed you when I woke up. Call me.

"Oh… is *that* how it is, now?" His sneering voice sent a tremor through her.

Oh God, no. The shudder worked her over from head to toe. *Please, don't let Noah get involved in this.*

He peered down into her eyes. "So you weren't just setting a trap for me last night… you're one of those shifter lovers who gets off on banging those freaks of nature."

She wanted to beg him to leave Noah alone, but she knew that would just make things worse. "I don't know what you're talking about." But even she could hear the tremor in her voice.

"Sure, you don't." He nodded and licked his lips, then scooped the phone off the desk. Her heart sank as he slipped it into his pocket. "This is going to be more fun than I thought."

That sent a chill through her that froze her solid.

His nasty grin was back. "I'll take care of Noah Wilding soon enough. But first, you're going to log me into the WildLove database and download all those shifters' real names and addresses onto a nice little drive for me."

Sourness rose up the back of Emily's throat. *How could she possibly stop this?*

He squeezed harder on one arm, then slid his other hand up to grasp her throat.

She couldn't help the whimper that came out of her mouth.

He leered down at her. "I don't have to shoot you to kill you," he said, breathing in her face. "And I don't *need* you, either. I was planning to hack in on my own, so all your pretty little neck is good for is saving me a little time. So what's it going to be, shifter-lover?"

A little time. She was scared—*scared to death*—but she needed more time to figure a way out of this. And some help to stop him from getting away with it. If he simply killed her and took what he wanted from the database, he'd never be caught... and hundreds, if not thousands, of shifter lives would be in danger. But if she went along with what he wanted, she could buy some precious time to find a way to stop him.

"I'll help you," she eeked out. It was hard to speak with his hand on her throat. "Please don't kill me."

He smirked and eased his hand back from choking her. "That's better." Then he shoved her down into her seat. "Now get me what I want. All of it—names, addresses, hookups, everything you have."

She nodded shakily and pointed to her dead screen. "I need power."

"Fix it!" he snarled.

She crawled under the desk, slowly, and plugged the station back in. Once she was back in her chair and her screen was booting up, she said, "That's a lot of data. It'll take some time."

He pulled a high-capacity drive out of his pocket and set it next to her keyboard. "Just get it done."

She would draw the process out as long as possible, and she would look for any opportunity to get away. But most importantly, she needed to get a message to Noah. Once she was inside the database, she could do it—set up a script, have it launch remotely, get a message to him somehow. But she had to be careful... this bomber had tech skills, and he was watching every move she made. She would have to be fast and would probably only get one chance.

She would have to make it count.

CHAPTER 13

Noah was just about to exit the Wylderide parking garage when Emily's text came.

It just pinged his phone and flashed by so he couldn't read it until he parked again. Then it took him forever to find it again, because it didn't come through as a normal message, but on the WildLove app instead. When he finally read it, he was glad he wasn't driving.

HELP. Bomber here at WildLove office.

He just stared at the phone for a long second. *Holy*

shit. Then he stabbed at the phone, quickly bringing up Owen's number and dialing.

"Hey, man, did you forget something?" Owen's voice was filled with laughter, and Noah could hear his cousin giggling in the background, but none of that mattered— he could barely hear them anyway over the roar of panic in his ears.

"The WildLove bomber has Emily," Noah gasped out.

Owen instantly sobered. *"What?"*

"I just got a text from her." Noah's voice was ramping up to panic. "God, Owen, he has her at the office. She went in early, and…" His throat was closing up. He shouldn't have brought her into this! And now she was in danger again.

"Where are you?" Owen was moving. Sounds in the background made it seem like he hauling ass.

"Parking garage," Noah choked out.

"Sit tight. I'll be right there." Owen's clipped, no-nonsense voice was reassuring, but Noah was just coming out of his panic-fueled fog. He had to go *now*. That maniac had *Emily*.

His throat opened up enough to let in some air. "I have to get over there—"

"I said *sit tight*. I'm on my way down. Meet me at the elevator."

"Okay. Right. Elevator." Noah put the car in gear and spun through the parking garage, heading back to the elevator.

"I'm hanging up to call for backup," Owen said through the phone. *"Do not* leave without me, Noah. Say it."

"Get the fuck down here, Owen," Noah ground out. It was killing him to not *already* be heading at high speed across downtown to the WildLove office.

"Copy that." Owen hung up.

In spite of the rock-hard grip Noah had on the steering wheel to keep himself from bolting, he was glad Owen was close by and on his way. He was ex-Army, just like Noah, plus he'd worked for Riverwise after they were both liberated from the cages. Barreling into this situation—probably a *hostage situation*, he realized with a horrible sinking feeling—would likely just get Emily killed. Noah needed a level head and backup, just like Owen said.

It took an interminable time, but it was probably only thirty seconds before Owen came sprinting out of the elevator. As soon as he was in the car, Noah stomped on the accelerator, and they pealed out of the parking garage.

"I called Riverwise," Owen said quickly but with a voice far calmer than Noah felt. "Daniel's on his way with a whole van full of pack members."

"Are they at the safehouse?" Noah asked as he screeched around a corner far too fast.

"Yes," Owen said tightly.

Which meant they were too far away to help. "We're on our own, then," Noah said, eyes glued to the road.

"Maybe." Owen pulled out two pistols and started loading one with ammo. "We get there, we case the situation, then we make that call. Deal?"

"I'm not risking Emily's life by waiting," Noah ground out as he took another corner.

"Understood." Owen started loading the second pistol.

The safehouse was an hour away from downtown. Maybe half that with Daniel driving like a madman. But Noah and Owen would be at the Seattle Shifters Dating Agency office in less than ten minutes, assuming they didn't crash or get pulled over.

"What do we know so far?" Owen asked, his voice still steady.

Nothing, Noah wanted to snap, but Owen's calm voice

was helping him keep his raging anger and guilt under control.

Instead, he steeled himself to brief Owen on anything that might help. "She was gone this morning when I woke up. Her text said she was heading to the office. Something about a new idea to track the bomber."

"Time?"

Noah nodded to his phone on the dash, so Owen picked it up and checked. "Okay, about an hour has elapsed since that first text. But I don't see the second one."

"That came through on the WildLove app. Under my NICK pseudonym."

Owen tapped the phone and took a moment to read the text. "Okay, not good." His voice was considerably more strained. "Hard to say when she sent it, but this just came through on your end. So, as of this text, we know she's holding it together, alive, and working on getting free. This is all positive, Noah."

"*Owen,*" he growled. A fucking murdering shifter-hater had his girl. There was nothing *positive* about that.

"Right. Shutting up, now."

Noah was sucking air between his teeth to hold it together. His wolf was howling to get out and tear apart whoever was holding Emily prisoner, but he had to keep his shit together to have any hope of rescuing her.

"Whoever has her," Noah said through his teeth, "has to be part of the hate group. She's calling him the bomber, so maybe it's actually *the* bomber."

"The guy from last night?"

"Yeah." Noah pushed through a nearly-red light. "He's been tech savvy from the jump, hacking the system, figuring out where the hookups were. Now he's at WildLove."

"Do you think he went in after her?"

"I don't know." Noah grimaced, trying to piece it together as they sped through downtown. "Why not go after her before? Why now?"

"If he's the bomber, then he must have seen her at the motel."

Noah slammed his hand against the steering wheel. *"Dammit!* I never should have involved her in this. What the fuck was I thinking?"

"Hey!" Owen's sharp tone cut through the fog clouding Noah's head. "You can feel like shit about this later, okay? Keep your head clear."

"Right. Okay." *Focus,* Noah. Jesus.

"So the bomber saw her, figured out she was a

WildLove programmer and went after her this morning… *after* he had figured out she wasn't killed in the blast," Owen reasoned. "What's his play on this? Is he holding her hostage? Is he hoping to ransom her? I mean, she managed to get a text to you, through the WildLove app. He hasn't killed her outright. She's still alive for some reason. Maybe he's not after her at all. Maybe she's hiding out under a desk somewhere."

"The database." The words came out soft as Noah realized what that meant. *"Oh shit.* Owen, he's after the database."

"The one with all the shifters in it." Owen just shook his head. "All right. Priority one, after making sure Emily is safe, of course, is to keep that database secure."

"Copy that." Noah pulled into the parking garage of Emily's building at a speed that had the tires screeching on the smooth concrete floor. He didn't bother parking, just pulled up to the elevators and sprinted from the car to the doors. Owen was close behind.

He would have run the stairs, but the elevator would get them there faster… only it was killing him to wait. Owen handed him a gun, which he held at the ready. The ride up was painfully slow, but the two of them came out, guns first, when they arrived at the floor that held the agency office. They cautiously approached the glass double doors, but there was no sign of anyone inside. Of course, they couldn't see past the reception area.

"What do you think?" Owen asked.

"I'm thinking we get the hell in there and find Emily." Noah's hand was already on the door.

Owen held up a hand to stop him. "All right, but we go quiet, yes? You know where her office is, so you lead the way. But he could be anywhere. Keep your eyes open."

Noah nodded and tried to pull open the door: *locked*.

"Fuck," he spit out. Then he tucked his gun in the back of his jeans and shifted his hands to the long, knife-like claws that were the curse of his new white wolf.

Owen did the same. "So much for quiet. Better make it fast, then."

Noah nodded, and together they sliced through the metal plates holding the doors locked tight. The screeching sound was horrific, and anyone inside had to know something was up. Noah shifted his hands back, yanked open the door, and barreled inside, pulling his gun back out along the way. Owen was right behind him as he hustled through the maze of cubicles, searching out Emily's desk.

The place was dead quiet. No one in sight. When they reached her office… it was empty. Her *Coffee is My Boyfriend* mug had tipped sideways and dumped its contents on the floor. Somehow that made it hard for him to breathe.

"He took her," Noah said, throat tight. "He grabbed her from her office."

Owen was checking the other cubicles, but there was nothing to see. "Emily?" he called out. There was no answer. "Is there a server bank around here somewhere?" he asked Noah.

"A what?" Noah blinked at him, his head fogged again. *Get it together!* he told himself.

"The place where they keep all the data servers, the computers," Owen said. "If he was after the database, maybe he took her there."

"Right. Good thinking. Back here." Noah led him past the cubicles to a large, heavily air-conditioned room in the center of the office. Emily had shown him the server room at one point. He pushed open the thick steel doors, revealing a dozen banks of tall, black metal servers. It was rack after rack of computational power, blinking with red and blue lights… but no people.

Noah listened over the soft hum of the climate

control and the machines, but there were no human sounds. "Emily?" he called, just to be sure. "Are you in here?"

But there was no reply.

"What the hell is that?" Owen pointed to a box at the end of the nearest server bank.

It was counting down something in luminescent red numerals.

A timer. With only seconds left.

Oh shit. "Bomb!" Noah shouted, hauling Owen away from the device and toward the door. "Move, move, move!"

But he didn't have to say it—they both slammed through the doors and ran for their lives. They barely reached the end of the cubicle area, when the blast ripped through the walls, sending fragments of computers, wiring, and plaster hurtling through the air. The concussive force threw them against the reception area doors, slamming them on the clear glass, but not breaking it.

Smoke and debris filled the air, and for the second time in twenty-four hours, Noah's ears were ringing from the shock wave of a bomb that was meant to kill him… but didn't.

Or maybe the bomber was just trying to wreak vengeance on WildLove.

Owen helped Noah to his feet, and they both stared blankly at the debris-filled air and the giant hole in the building where the server farm used to be.

"He just blew up WildLove," Noah said, struggling to piece it together.

"And almost us," Owen said under his breath. "That was too damn close." He brushed off some of the debris clinging to his shirt.

Then Noah realized something. "The bomber must have set the timer just before he left." He turned and slammed his fist against the glass door, making it shake. "We just missed him!"

Owen frowned. "And Emily's not here, so he took her with him."

"But *where?*" Noah asked, anguish creeping into his voice.

Suddenly the entrance of the agency was flung open, and a half dozen of the Riverwise pack dashed through the double glass doors, with his brother in the lead. Daniel's eyes were wide, but they quickly took in the fact that Noah and Owen were still upright, and the alarm on his face stepped down a level.

Owen pushed open the interior glass doors to meet him.

Daniel frowned at the office past their shoulders. "Jesus Christ. What happened here?"

"We just missed the bomber," Noah said in a tight voice.

"Looks like he just missed you," Daniel said with a scowl.

"He still has Emily." Noah couldn't help the growl in his voice.

Owen's hand landed on Noah's shoulder. "Maybe we can pull something off the surveillance video. Security has to have something."

"Police are going to be crawling all over this place in five minutes and locking everything down." Noah ran both hands through his hair and came back with bits of drywall. "We've got to *move.*"

"Copy that," Daniel said, waving them away from the blast scene. "But even if we get an ID on the car, Noah…" His lips pinched together, but Noah knew what he was leaving unsaid.

That they had no idea where the bomber was taking Emily. And now that the bomber presumably had whatever he came for, blowing up everything once he was done, there was no telling what he would do with the lead programmer for WildLove. That idea twisted Noah's stomach in a knot so tight he could barely breathe. A hostage is worthless, a liability, once their kidnapper has what they want. *Why did he take Emily?*

"Let's go," Noah said. He was the first to the elevator doors. He didn't care what the odds were of finding Emily alive, he sure as hell wasn't giving up... not until she was safe again.

Or the bomber was shredded under Noah's claws.

CHAPTER 14

E mily was terrified.

The shaking of her hands was visible, even though they were duct-taped together. And she had to clamp her teeth shut to keep them from chattering with every bump in the road. She couldn't help the full-body shudder every time the bomber leered at her from the driver's seat next to her. He was taking her somewhere… and there was nothing that could possibly be good about that.

Worst of all, she'd managed to endanger Noah in

calling for help. When she'd slipped that text to him, she'd had no idea the bomber—*Richard,* although that couldn't be his real name—was going to blow up the whole office. Once she'd downloaded the database to his portable drive, he'd forced her to watch while he set the explosives to take down the server farm. She couldn't fathom why he *hated* so much—her, shifters, the entire WildLove company. It wasn't like her life was perfect. Far from it. But it was beyond her comprehension how someone's soul could be so dark, so filled with anger and loathing, that they would want to destroy so many people's lives, both by killing them outright and by destroying their jobs. She prayed Noah didn't actually come for her and that he escaped the bomber's trap.

But she doubted she would do the same.

In spite of the terror running through her body, her mind didn't give up. It was still whirling and clicking along, trying to figure out a way to escape. Maybe it was just her survival instinct kicking in—whatever it was, she'd considered and discarded a half dozen ideas, including wrenching open the car door and jumping out to avoid whatever fate awaited her at their destination. But she couldn't force herself to take that last desperate option.

Not yet.

The bomber had brought his black bag of bomb tricks along with him. It sat on the seat behind her. She'd seen him rifle through it, and she thought she saw him slip her phone into the bag along with the drive with the WildLove data on it, although she wasn't sure. If she could manage to get the drive out of the bag and toss it out the window, or destroy it somehow, that would at least spare the shifters he would no doubt target next. Or if she could get hold of her phone, she could text Noah for help again. Or simply call the police. But Noah would come faster. If he wasn't already in pieces.

Angry, frightened tears blurred her vision... but she couldn't afford that right now. She reached up to wipe them away with her tape-bound hands, loathing the fact that the bomber noticed and smirked at her obvious fear. He was getting off on it. She choked back the hot anger that threatened to bring more tears and stared straight ahead, trying not to give him the satisfaction of watching her break down. As her vision cleared, she saw they were turning into the parking lot of a seedy motel. They'd been in the car less than ten minutes, but another shudder ran through her as she realized *this* was where they were headed. Visions of the explosion from the night before—

the one in another motel room that she and Noah barely survived—barraged her mind.

She looked to the bomber. His smirk was firmly in place. "Honey, we're here!" he said with an insanely cheery voice.

Her stomach heaved.

"Don't worry, I'll be right back for you," he said, reaching to the back seat and his black bag. He came back with the roll of duct tape, grabbed her already bound hands, and pulled her toward him. "Can't have you running off while I check in, honey!" He looped another series of wrappings around her hands then bound them to the steering wheel. His eyes sparkled as he ran his hand along her hair, pushing it away from where it had fallen across her face. A wave of revulsion threatened to choke her. Then he climbed out of the car and strode toward the motel office.

Presumably to get them a room.

Once she was there, she was a dead woman. She knew this.

A wave of fear animated her, and she thrashed against the steering wheel. Surprisingly, the quick tape job didn't hold—it slipped a little as she struggled, freeing one edge. Using her teeth, she grabbed the loose piece and peeled it back. A frantic ten seconds later she was free.

She should run.

A quick look at the glassed-in office told her the bomber would see her. And come after her. Even if she ran, she wouldn't escape. Maybe the manager would notice. Maybe not. She should get her phone out of the bag and call for help instead. She had enough time to run or call, but not both.

No time to decide.

She twisted between the two front bucket seats, reaching for the black bag. The angle was terrible, and her hands were still bound by the tape, but she managed to work the zipper open. Fumbling through it, her fingers quickly found her phone. She willed her shaking hands to calm enough to text Noah. *Cassidy Motel.* That was all she had time for. Then she wiped the screen and threw the phone back in the bag, terrified the bomber would return to find her in the middle of texting. When she was sure he was still inside, she fished for the drive next. Amazingly, her fingers found its smooth surface, and she pulled it free of the tangle of wires, electronic boxes, tools and other things filling the bag. There was no time to throw the drive from the car—not that she could even get the window down without the keys—so she leaned forward and stashed it under the seat instead. Maybe hiding it would be enough to make him think he'd lost it. She shoved the drive back as far as she could, giving it an extra kick with the heel of her foot. Just as she looked up, hair flying wild around her, the bomber came striding out of the motel office, anger blazing on his face when he saw her.

She shrank against the passenger door as he yanked open the driver's side and climbed in.

He glared at the tattered tape dangling from the steering wheel. "You're a slippery little thing, aren't you?"

Her stomach heaved again with the way his eyes raked over her body.

He threw the car into reverse, pulled away from the office, then drove around to the back of the motel, out of sight of the road, the office, and just about anyone who might notice he had a kidnapped woman in his car. He stopped at the very last room at the end of a long, two-story line of them, parking near the forested lot that backed up to the motel. Her heart pounded as he grabbed the black bag and got out of the car.

Run, her mind was screaming, but she waited until he got to her side of the car and started to open her door. Then she lifted her legs and kicked hard against the door, banging it against him and sending him tumbling back. She struggled to get out of the car with her hands bound, and she didn't get a dozen feet before his arms clamped hard around her. She struggled and tried to kick him, but he quickly had her back pinned against him, his hand clasped around her throat, choking her.

"Keep struggling, and I'll kill you right here," he hissed in her ear.

Black spots swam in front of her eyes.

She stopped struggling.

The pressure eased on her throat enough that she could get air. She gasped, heaving air into her lungs as he hauled her toward the room. His hand was still on her throat, holding her tight, as he fussed with the lock, kicked the door open, and pulled her inside.

She thought her heart might just quit then.

Or maybe she simply wished it would.

He dragged her to the bed in the middle of the room. It had a headboard with posts. He slung the black bag on the bed and pulled out the tape again. Breath was still heaving in and out of her, but she had no will to fight him anymore. He bound one wrist to the post on one side, then made some kind of rope with the tape and tied her other wrist to the far post. She was strung between them, barely able to move, hung up like he was crucifying her on the bed.

God, she prayed whatever he had in mind would end fast. But the way he licked his lips when he surveyed his work made tears leak out of the corners of her eyes.

Explosives were sounding better all the time.

And maybe she should have jumped out of the car.

At least there was the possibility he wouldn't find the drive she'd hidden under the seat. Maybe. She hoped her death would count for something—saving that many shifters, that many innocent people, almost made whatever she would have to endure before the end worthwhile.

She watched the bomber with a dull sort of awareness as he fished materials out of his bag. He was whistling happily as he lined items up on the dresser opposite the bed where she was trussed up like a sacrificial lamb. It wasn't until he started taping something to the bedposts next to her bound wrists that she recognized the gray bricks and shiny control boxes for what they were—*bombs.* Just like the ones he had set up on the servers. They weren't active yet—or at least the timers weren't counting down—but he wasn't finished, either. Two more were placed on either side of the window and two more next to the door. With the amount of explosives he had deployed around the room, Emily wouldn't be surprised if it took down the entire motel... or at least the far end of the building.

The last item to come out of the bag was a laptop, which he set on the dresser and tapped furiously at for a long while. She was afraid he would notice the missing drive, but he didn't seem to. She couldn't understand what he was doing at all. Pulling up data on his laptop for some bizarre reason right in the middle of this elaborate setup to kill her? But as the minutes dragged on, she just didn't care. Her mind was finally shutting down, refusing to try to figure out the evil that was this person, this hater, this awful being who only knew how to hurt and destroy.

Some vague time later, when the bomber finally stepped away from the laptop, she could see the red recording light was lit up.

Oh God. The terror that had been glossed over and numbed out by her defeat surged back up again. She'd seen the videos the Wolf Hunter had made before. There was the original doxing, the exposing of all the names and addresses of the shifters in the River and Wilding packs. Then the awful dismemberment videos. Then the livestreaming of a shifter's almost-death.

What in God's name was he planning for her? And was this the Wolf Hunter himself?

She watched with wide eyes as he pulled a mask from the depths of the bag and slipped it over his face. When he turned to her, she saw the mask was a plain face, just an average person… some guy whose average-guy-looks were stamped into plastic. Not at all like the previous Wolf Hunter masks. But it obscured the bomber's real face, and that was all he was after. Because apparently he was planning to walk out of the motel room before it— and her—blew into tiny bits.

"Emily Jones," he intoned like the judge at her execution, "your work has allowed hundreds, if not thousands, of shifters to pollute our gene pool, seducing our women to spread their vile seed."

"You're *insane*," she spat at him. "WildLove brought people together, consenting adults. It was all about *love*, not hate. Not like *you.*"

He chuckled darkly. "WildLove was about depraved sexual acts, nothing more. By making it easy for shifters to prey on human weakness, you're guilty of crimes against humankind. And now you're going to pay for it."

He was speaking to the audience on the video he was

recording.

"And livestreaming my death isn't depraved?" She shoved all her loathing into one, intense glare.

The bomber edged forward, careful not to block the camera's view of her strung up on the bed. "Not livestream. Delayed broadcast. It's caching with a delay, but don't worry, it'll broadcast as soon as we're done here."

Sourness climbed the back of her throat. "You won't get away with this."

He laughed again, then strode to the front of the bed, standing next to her and staring down through the small eyeholes of his mask. He grabbed hold of her chin, tipping it up so she was forced to look at him. "You'll pay for your crimes, but first we're going to have a little fun, Emily. A little lesson to those human women who think they want to share a bed with a shifter." Then he released her chin to caress her cheek.

She wrenched her face away, but her heart was about to pound out of her chest, which was heaving again in a desperate attempt to get air. *No, no, no… he was going to…* she flashed back to her uncle, five years ago, grunting and sweating on top of her, forcing her legs apart, hurting her… The idea of enduring that again before the bomber finally blew her up, all before an audience…

Her stomach heaved again, but it nothing came up. She willed herself to get sick all over him and the bed, but her whole body was locking down, closing up, folding in on itself.

The bomber grabbed her cheek and forced her to look his way, but her eyes were already glazed over. Her mind was fleeing, seeking escape, running from this reality. There was nothing left but pain and horror here.

She barely felt his hands on her hair, her body, tugging at her clothes.

The sound his zipper made when he lowered it only registered as a distant grating.

There were other sounds, but she ignored them. Her eyes were already closed. Her mind was already gone. She would die soon. She knew this. And as her mind went far, far away, she had only a single, solitary thought that went with her:

She should have jumped from the car.

CHAPTER 15

Noah was going out of his mind.

Owen and Daniel were scouring the security tapes, the rest of the pack was waiting around, getting twitchier by the moment, but Noah was genuinely losing his sanity. Images of Emily, bleeding out on a tacky linoleum floor, kept popping into his head and blocking out every other sight, sound, or thought. Only he knew it wasn't her... it was his mother, wrists slit and life ebbing out into the puddle of broken glass and whiskey on the floor next to her. A full-color image from his childhood was haunting him... all because he was standing around the WildLove office complex, unable to do a damn thing about finding Emily, much less save her.

Noah blinked away the image. *Focus.*

He checked his WildLove app for the hundredth time, but there were no more messages. Just as he was putting away his phone, another notification popped up.

Emily.

He jabbed at the notice before it could disappear, and her full message appeared. It was only two words, but they slammed into his heart.

"She's at the Cassidy Motel!" he shouted.

The room stilled.

"What do you have?" Daniel asked from his spot next to the security monitors.

"Emily texted me her location!" Noah yelled, already halfway to the door. He sprinted out of the security office and bypassed the elevator to stampede down the two flights to the parking garage. His car was still illegally parked in front of the elevators. He was in the driver's seat and ready to tear out of the garage, having no clue where the Cassidy Motel even was, when Daniel and Owen spilled out of the stairwell and ran for his car.

Noah forced himself to wait the two seconds it would take for them to reach it.

"Go!" Owen said as soon as they were in.

Noah slammed the car into drive. "I need directions!"

"On it," Daniel said, riding shotgun and whipping out his phone.

As Daniel directed him out of the parking garage, Noah spoke over him. "How far?" he demanded.

"About ten minutes cross-town," Daniel said, voice taut. "It's a shitty little place at the edge of town."

His mind was just now catching up to where they were going. "Holy shit, it's a motel. Why would he take her there?"

Daniel and Owen exchanged a look but said nothing.

"Fuck!" Noah slammed his hand against the steering wheel. He knew as well as they did that no matter what it was, it was bad. The bomber could kill her there and be long gone before anyone found her. "I am *not* letting him kill her." *Not again. Not like before.* His mind was snarled up so badly in this. His heart was pounding so loudly he could hear it in his ears, a steady drumbeat of rage that had been pounding through him ever since he'd been a child.

"Right at the light," Daniel said, holding the dash as

Noah blew through the red light and took the turn at top speed.

The car was silent after that except for Daniel calling out directions and the car tires screeching around corners. Each heartbeat felt like it was pulsing louder in Noah's ears, and it seemed as if they would never reach the motel, but long minutes later, he careened into the parking lot. Owen had to hold him back from strangling the attendant at the front desk when he balked at giving out the room number, but the murderous look in Noah's eyes must have convinced him.

Noah didn't wait for the room key, just took off for his car once he had the number and sped around to the back of the motel. There was a single car parked at the end, outside the door of the room. As soon as he was out of his own car, Noah had his claws out, ready to shred the door. He was tearing into it, maniacally, before Owen and Daniel even reached him. Daniel pulled him back, and Noah almost swung and cut him, but he checked his swing at the last moment, just as Owen kicked the door in.

All three of them rushed the door… then froze.

A man in a mask cowered next to Emily—she was tied to a bed, surrounded by explosives.

"Stay back!" the man screamed. "Or I'll blow us all!" He held a box to Emily's chest, a gray brick of something with a silver-box detonator, just like the one strapped to the computers at WildLove. The man was using her body and the bed as cover. Identical explosives were bound to the posts by Emily's hands.

She wasn't moving.

Her pants were down to her ankles, but her panties were still in place. That fact sent rage coursing through Noah, but seeing that her eyes were *still* closed spiked him with terror. She was utterly motionless, even with the bomber shouting at her side, almost like she was already...

"Is she alive?" Noah's mouth tasted of ash as the words left it. Because if the bomber had already killed her, Noah would simply call the man's bluff and shred him to pieces.

Before the bomber could respond, Emily answered his question by blinking open her beautiful eyes and peering at him. It was almost like she didn't think he was real, or maybe she couldn't really see him, crowding the doorway with Owen and Daniel at his back.

"If you want her to stay alive, *shifter,*" the man spat at him, "back the fuck out of here!"

There was no way that was happening. *Emily was alive*... and Noah wasn't leaving without her.

"Are you all right?" he asked her. His throat was still stinging with the bitter taste of fear—fear that he had lost her, that he'd been too late—but it was fading fast under his determination to get her free.

She frowned at him. "Noah?" Then she blinked rapidly, and her voice hiked up. "Noah, the door and the window, they're rigged. Explosives. Don't come any closer!"

There was no way that was happening, either. But Noah couldn't see a way out of this stalemate. If he lunged for the bomber, he might trigger the detonator he had pressed against Emily's chest... and Noah couldn't take that risk. Even in his wolf form, he couldn't move fast enough.

Daniel pressed a gun flat against Noah's back, reminding him that they were armed. Noah waved him back. The bomber was too close to Emily—there was far more of her body to hit than his. They weren't exactly far away, and Noah was a decent shot, but still... he might miss.

"Use what you know," Owen said out of the corner of his mouth.

Noah frowned and glanced at him. What was he talking about?

"No one deserves it more," Owen said, holding his gaze.

Suddenly, Noah knew exactly what he meant. He quickly held his hands up.

"I'm unarmed," Noah said to the bomber, taking a half-step into the room.

The man twitched, his eyes wide. "Stay back!"

"I'll make a trade," Noah said, edging slightly closer. He had no idea if this would work. He'd only done it once. "Me for the girl."

"Noah, no!" Emily gasped.

Noah kept his eyes glued to the bomber. Then he reached for the man, but not physically. This reach was magical… that same energy that was coiled inside him, writhing and angry, like his wolf only stronger.

The man's eyes narrowed. "I don't want *you*. I want safe passage out of here!" He nodded to where Owen and Daniel still crowded the door.

"You want out. I want the girl. We make a trade." Noah edged forward as he spoke, hands still out. He didn't know how close he had to be. In Afghanistan, the whole thing was over in an instant. This was the first time he'd even tried to reach out as he had before, intuitively…

"Clear those guys out!" the man waved jerkily at the door, panic showing in the whites of his eyes behind the mask.

Noah waved Daniel and Owen back as well. His brother frowned like Noah was crazy, but Owen tugged Daniel back from the threshold. Noah edged even further into the room, and suddenly he could feel the man's presence—an energy, like a malevolent storm, that called to his inner beast.

His inner witch.

"You." Noah raised his arm to point at the man. "Need to die."

Even under the mask, Noah could see the man's eyes go wide. Then a crackling streak of blue energy leaped from Noah's outstretched finger, formed an arc across the air, and nailed the man straight through the forehead. The sound of it split the air like lightning, and Emily shrieked. But an instant later, the man was gone. Noah didn't have to look… he could feel the bomber's energy dissipate, and he knew the man, his mask, and all his vile intentions had been reduced to ash.

In an instant, Noah leaped across the room to the

bed. Emily was frozen, terrified, eyes wide and freaked out, but she didn't recoil away from him. He lifted the bomb off her chest, then shifted a single finger into a razor sharp claw and slashed at the tape binding her. Once his blade was safely returned to the form of a gentle human hand, he scooped her up from the bed. She curled right into him, and he tucked her close... then he ran. He didn't know if the explosives were rigged to blow by themselves, on a timer, or just on a switch, but he wasn't taking any chances. He didn't even bother with the car, he just kept running until he reached the end of the motel building and had Emily safely away from whatever blast might be triggered.

She was shaking all over, and when Noah set her down on her feet, he didn't really let her go. He held her close, peering at her face, thrilled beyond measure that she was standing here, in his arms, all in one piece.

Her pants were still tangled around her legs.

He dropped to one knee and gently brought them up again, holding her close, protective even now, as she buttoned them with shaking fingers.

"Please tell me he didn't hurt you," Noah said, his voice soft.

She shook her head back and forth, a jittery motion,

but definitely a *no*. "He was going to…" She swallowed and looked up at him. "He would have. If you hadn't stopped him."

Those words… Noah couldn't speak with the emotion that was welling up in him. Maybe his grandfather was a witch. Maybe Noah was a witch, too, or at least some kind of hybrid. But if all he ever did with that power was what he did tonight—*save Emily*—then everything, every rejection by his family and his pack, every shame that would be coming his way, would be worth it.

Emily was looking over his shoulder, back at the motel room. "What you did back there…" She brought her wondering gaze back to him. "How did you do that?"

He grimaced. But it was all going to come out sooner or later. Mostly sooner, now that he'd revealed himself to not only Emily but his brother as well. "I'm not just a wolf, Emily."

Her eyes went wide, but she just nodded. "You're a white wolf."

He huffed a small laugh. "Yeah. That's part of it."

The crunch of car tires rolled up behind him. Daniel and Owen had brought the car to them.

Noah turned back to her. His hands were still gently holding her up, but her shaking was starting to calm. He let her go. "Basically, I'm part witch, part wolf," he said quickly, before his brother's hard looks from inside the car coalesced into a determination to grill him on what had just happened. "I'll explain it all to you later. Right now, how about we just get out of here?"

She nodded, dazedly. He turned, his hand on her elbow, not touching her too much, in case that wasn't something she wanted anymore, given that she knew what he was now. He guided her toward the car. She stopped suddenly before getting in.

"Wait." She turned her pretty blue eyes on him. "The WildLove database. He made me copy it for him, but I hid it under the front seat of the car. I was trying to fight him, but…" She seemed frustrated that somehow she hadn't been able to thwart a shifter-hater and save legions of shifters all on her own. Even though she'd nearly done so.

He couldn't help touching her cheek, gently, just once. "Of course, you did." He looked to Owen, who had gotten out of the car soon enough to hear. "Owen?"

"On it," he said, then turned to trot back to where the bomber's car was parked.

"He was also recording the whole… the whole thing he had planned," Emily said, her voice wavering and some of the shaking coming back.

Noah's chest squeezed tight. "He *recorded* it?" Not only was the bastard planning to rape her, but he was *filming it?* Noah had an urgent need to kill him all over again.

Emily nodded fervently. "On the laptop. Delayed broadcast. Noah…" She grabbed his arm. "It probably recorded what you did."

He just stared at her for a moment, amazed: she was worried about *him*.

Noah turned to where Owen's form was just about to disappear into the motel room. "Owen!" he called. "Grab that laptop!"

Owen waved and went inside.

Noah turned back to her and smiled. "You just saved me a whole lot of trouble."

She frowned. "I'm pretty sure I caused you more than enough trouble before that."

He just shook his head. And he couldn't resist bringing her in for a hug, not least because she still had some tremble in her.

"You have no idea how glad I am to see you in one piece," he whispered into her hair. Then he forced himself to let her go. He gestured to the car. "Come on. Let's get you out of here."

She nodded and climbed into the back seat of his car.

Noah ignored his brother's steely-eyed looks and climbed in after her.

There would be time for all the explanations later.

CHAPTER 16

Emily had never eaten so much in her life.

"Here, take another pancake." That was Mama River, the matriarch of the River pack family, pushing yet another fluffy, buttermilk slice of heaven on her. She'd already had five.

"They're amazing, Mrs. River, seriously," Emily said. "Best pancakes I've ever had. But I think I might burst."

The graceful smile on Mama River's face was more *satisfaction* than flattered by her compliment.

Noah hurried into the room and cased the situation with a quick look. "Mama River, what are you doing?" He looked very concerned.

Mama River wasn't his mother, but she apparently hovered over everyone at the River pack safehouse like they were her adopted children. She gave Noah a chiding scowl. "Trying to make sure this girl is properly fed."

Noah scowled right back. "I just asked you to watch over her for a minute, not force feed her." He had disappeared to "take care of something" for about ten minutes, but other than that brief absence, he had stuck fast by Emily's side every minute of the last couple hours. After he had plucked her from a horrible fate at the hands of the bomber, they had quickly left the motel and driven up into the beautiful mountains outside Seattle, finally ending up here, at the River family estate. The shock from the traumatic events of the morning was starting to wear off, only to be replaced with the shock of being in a sprawling ranch *filled* with shifters. They were mostly men, and all outrageously gorgeous. It befuddled her senses, being surrounded by so many insanely hot wolves, especially *famous* ones she'd only previously read about in the papers. And now she was stuffed with pancakes and easy acceptance from Mama River as well.

The past twenty-four hours were easily the worst and best of Emily's life.

"Have you actually looked at this girl?" Mama River protested, her ire seeming to rise with Noah's objections. "She's as white as a ghost and probably still in shock. She needs a proper feeding."

Emily held up a hand to stop them. She didn't want to be the source of any trouble. "Mama River's right. I needed it." Emily made a show of rising up from the table. "But any more, and you're going to have to carry me home, Noah."

The expression on his face wasn't quite a smile—more like a mischievous hunger—and it sent a thrill through her. She'd caught him looking at her like that ever since he'd rescued her from the bomber, and every time it reminded her of the passion they'd shared just the night before. It sent heat coursing to her lady parts, which were aching for more of him. But that had to be over now… right? Even with everything that had happened, he was still… *magical.* Even if she wasn't sure exactly what flavor of magic Noah possessed anymore.

And she was still just a human.

"I would love to carry you to your room, Ms. Jones," Noah said, his not-smile getting even more mischievous.

"My room?" she asked, frowning and throwing a glance at Mama River.

"Ah, well," Mama River sighed. "It's a good thing I fueled you up, my dear." She rose from the table and started gathering up the dishes.

Emily had no idea what she meant. "I'm fine, really, Noah. I can go back to the city now, I just need a ride—"

"Absolutely not." Noah stepped closer, took her by the elbow, and ushered her out of the kitchen.

"The extra pancakes will be in the fridge!" Mama River called after them.

"I really don't need a room," Emily protested as Noah led her through the great room of the estate and toward the stairs by the front door. "I don't want to inconvenience anyone."

"The very last thing you are is an inconvenience," he said quietly in her ear.

There were several shifters gathered in the great room, and their stares followed Emily and Noah across the room. Her rescuers, Daniel and Owen, were among them, but also the River brothers, Jaxson, Jace, and Jared. To a one, they were all ridiculously sexy, each in their own way. With them all together, Emily could see how Noah, even with his rippling shifter muscles and broad shoulders, was still the fresh-faced baby of the bunch.

Being in the presence of all that male hotness had her head swimming.

Noah made a very soft sound that was almost a growl, and his grip on her elbow tightened a little as he directed her up the stairs. "I've got a room ready for you," he said quietly, but his voice definitely carried over the hush of the room. "You can stay as long as you like, but you really do need to stay for a day or two, at least until we're sure it's okay for you to return to the city. Not to mention the office." By the time he finished speaking, they'd made it to the top of the stairs, and out of view of their onlookers below. Noah stopped her in the empty hallway. "Please don't fight me on this, Emily," he said even more quietly. "Please say you'll stay, at least for a little while." He was beseeching her with his eyes as if he thought she might actually say *no*.

"Of course," she said. "If you're sure it's no trouble."

He pulled back a little. "Your room is this way." His hand was back on her elbow as he directed her down the hall. He seemed to be doing that a lot since they left the motel, touching her elbow or her face or the small of her back, staying physically close to her like he was reassuring himself that she was still there. She had to reassure herself, too, every once in a while, stopping for a moment to actually look around and acknowledge that she'd survived. She had been so ready to die, it was still a shock to her that she hadn't.

And she had yet to properly thank Noah for saving her life.

When he swung open the door to her room, she was utterly charmed by it. The entire estate was decorated in a very rustic style—rough-hewn log walls, sturdy furniture that seemed carved from the forest surrounding it, and warm colors of orange and brown and a clear white that made everything feel cozy yet elegant. Her room had a slightly feminine touch with a snow-white comforter and small lace trimmings on the curtains, but otherwise, it had that same home-spun feel as the rest of the house.

She turned to face Noah just as he closed the door behind him.

"Emily," he began, "I wanted to tell you something—"

She cut him off by stepping forward and sliding her hands up around his neck. "And I wanted to tell *you* something, too." But instead of saying her *thank you*, she lifted up on her tip-toes to reach his lips and kiss him. She had planned to just give him a light kiss on the lips, then pull back and tell him how amazingly grateful she was to have him in her life, even if for just a short time, but once she was there... Noah's hands found her back and pressed her body against his rock-hard chest. She couldn't help melting against him as his lips consumed hers, his tongue probing gently into her mouth, then more urgently as she opened for him and kissed him back. His hands bunched in her hair and pressed her closer, and suddenly her heart was racing, wanting more than it should from him.

After a moment, he broke the kiss, breathing hard and not going far from her lips. "I like your *something* much better than mine," he said, breathlessly.

She swallowed, trying to catch her breath, but he was still holding her so intimately, it was impossible. "I just wanted to thank you for saving my life."

"Oh," he said. "Right." His hold on her loosened, and she instantly missed it. Then he touched her again, just a finger running along her hair and tucking it behind her ear. "I just can't help myself around you, Em. And with all these other shifters staring at you... I told you before, you bring out my alpha. And I can't help wanting you all to myself."

Her heart swelled with that, and it threatened to break

her. Didn't he know the effect those words would have on her? "You risked your life to save mine. You came for me when I thought everything was lost. Noah, there's only one wolf in this house I could ever want to be with."

He closed his eyes briefly, like her words were causing him pain, which she didn't understand at all. She touched her fingers to his cheek, and he opened his eyes again.

"Except I'm not a wolf, am I?" he whispered.

She frowned. "Tell me about what happened back there. In the motel room."

He nodded and stepped back, but didn't go far. He led her over to the bed, and they sat down together. It seemed to take a moment for him to find the right words.

"My biological grandfather was a white wolf," he said, not meeting her gaze. "It's the family scandal because he was the beta of my grandfather's pack, and he was sleeping with the alpha's mate."

Emily leaned back. "I thought mates had a magical bond…" She swallowed. Was everything she knew about shifters wrong? "Doesn't the mating bond prevent that?"

He lifted his gaze to meet hers. "Normally, yes. The magic in the mating bond ties the mated wolves together for life, and generally speaking, nothing can interfere with that. But my biological grandfather, the white wolf, wasn't a wolf at all. He was a witch. And apparently his magic was so powerful, he could defeat the mating bond, steal my grandfather's mate, and impregnate her with his child… all without the alpha knowing." Noah gritted his teeth for a moment. "He was a real stand-up guy. So you can understand why being related to him isn't exactly something I was happy to discover."

Emily shook her head, confused. "You didn't always know this?"

"No." Noah sighed. "Before the experiments, I thought the only asshole in my lineage was my own father. I was an ordinary shifter—my wolf was brown-coated with normal claws and no insane magical powers. But the serums triggered something in me, brought out some kind of recessive side. The experiments were what turned me into a white wolf and exposed who I really am." He took a breath. "And as you saw this morning, I've got this… *magic*… inside me. My white wolf isn't a wolf at all. I'm a witch, Emily." He seemed horribly distraught by this, as if it was the worst thing that could possibly happen to him… which completely perplexed her.

"And this is bad?" she asked gently.

"*Yes,* this is bad," he said, angry, but it wasn't directed at her, not really. "My brother is horrified—I haven't even talked about it with him yet. The pack doesn't know what to do with me. And I'm pretty sure I just permanently freaked out every wolf I know." He hesitated, and then his voice softened. "And I'll understand if you don't want anything to do with now. I'm not the wolf you thought I was."

She peered at him, amazed, and wondering if he was really serious with this. "You're not the wolf I thought you were?"

"I know you thought all wolves were something special—"

"You're kidding me, right?" Now *she* was angry… and at him, although not really. Just at this silly part of him that thought this amazing ability was something to be ashamed of.

He looked confused. "No, I'm not kidding—"

"All right, you need to shut up right now and listen to me." She scowled at him to let him know she was serious.

He pressed his lips together and just looked at her like she was crazy. Which she probably was, but that was beside the point. She was *not* going to let him think he was anything less than magnificent in her eyes.

Emily got up on her knees on the bed and held

Noah's cheeks gently in her hands so she could stare straight into his eyes. "Noah Wilding, you are the most amazing and brave man I have ever met. You are selfless and good. I don't care who your grandfather was or what he did. I don't care what kind of magical creature you are, although for the record, your white wolf form is brilliant and gorgeous, and I think you're entirely *wolf* in all the ways that count. And your human form is so insanely hot, I can barely keep my hands off you. If you've got some magical power beyond that—this ability to shoot freaking blue fire from your fingertips—the only thing I need to know is that you used your magic to save me from the worst thing that's ever happened to me. And that includes when my uncle raped me five years ago." Tears were welling up in her eyes, and raw emotion was sweeping through her at the expression on Noah's face— a mixture of awe and wonder that made her want to weep—but she pressed on. Because she had to get it all out before she dissolved into a puddle of tears. "You're everything I thought wolves would be and so much more. And you've changed my life, just as I knew you would."

Noah reached for her and pulled her into the sweetest, most tender kiss she'd ever felt. "Emily, I want you so badly, I can hardly stand it."

Tears threatened to leak from her eyes with those words. "If you don't make love to me right now, I think I might actually cry."

He pulled her down into his lap and kissed her again and again. His hands held her tight, like he thought she might accidentally slip away.

Then he pulled back and gently touched his forehead to hers, closing his eyes as he spoke. "Once isn't enough for me. Or twice. I want you forever, Em."

Her breath caught in her throat, and she struggled to speak. "Forever?"

He opened his eyes, and they were blazing at her. "I want to claim you for my own. For always. It's entirely selfish, but I can't stand the thought of anyone else having you. I can't stand the idea of not having you always in my life."

"But I…" Her mind was reeling. He *knew* she was human. What was he saying? "You deserve someone who's a shifter. A *true* mate. I mean, I didn't think humans and wolves could even…" She ran out of words because the possibility was blanking out all her thoughts.

He touched her cheek. "They can. And they do. But I shouldn't ask this of you. It's not fair. The magic would only be one way—my magic in your blood, binding you to me. You don't have the magic to make the bond work both ways. I shouldn't ask you to even consider it, but I'm just stupid lucky to have found someone as amazing as you, and I can't let you go without at least trying. There's no woman on this earth I want more, Emily. If we mated, you would always be magically bound to me. All I can offer in return is my promise to honor that bond and do everything in my power to love you and keep you safe all the days of my life."

"You really…" She was entirely choked up. "You really want this? With me?"

"God, yes… if you'll have me." His eyes were pleading with her again.

She threw her arms around him. "Yes. Yes!"

He growled and pulled her into another kiss, pivoting them down into the soft puff of the comforter so that his deliciously hot body was on top of hers. "Say it again."

"Yes!" She grinned up at him.

"Say you want me." His eyes were blazing again.

She tamed her smile and gave him a dead-serious look that was equal to the pledge that was bursting in her heart. "I want to be your mate, Noah Wilding."

His growl this time was deep in his chest as he dove

into kissing her. His hands were everywhere on her, squeezing and caressing and powerfully possessive, like he wanted to grab hold of every part of her and stake his claim. It turned her on like nothing she'd ever felt.

Noah Wilding wanted her for a mate.

The idea was still ricocheting around in her head, causing awe and mayhem wherever it hit. She had no idea what it really meant, and it felt like flinging herself off a high cliff into some unknown heaven below, but there was absolutely no way she would say *no* to any of it.

"Clothes. Off. Now." Noah growled in her ear as he tugged at her shirt and jeans.

She helped him slide them off. When she was down to her panties and bra, she grabbed at his clothes to insist he play fair. He pulled his shirt off for her, but then his hands were busy on her again. He shifted one finger into a sharp blade, just like when he cut her bindings free in the motel, only now he sliced her bra free from her body.

"I hope you weren't fond of that one," he whispered in her ear before sliding down to take one of her rock-hard nipples into his mouth. His now-human hand slid into her panties, quickly finding the wetness pooling there. He groaned, and she arched up from the bed. He was already pleasuring her so intensely, just with this hot mouth and strong fingers, that her body was literally aching for him.

Her hands dug into his hair as he kissed a line across her belly, slicing her panties free and dipping his head between her legs. *"Oh, God, Noah."* She bucked into him, but he held her hips to the bed, nudging her legs apart and using his tongue in a way that was making stars swarm in front of her eyes. With one hand on his head, encouraging him, and the other clawing at the comforter, she came hard and fast, rocking against him and the insane pleasure he was giving her.

She was pretty sure she was hyperventilating.

He came up grinning. "Did you like that?"

"No," she gasped, barely able to breathe. "It was terrible. Please do it again. Immediately."

He chuckled, but it quickly dissolved into a moan as he slid his hot body, skin-on-skin against hers. He still had his jeans on.

"Pants. Off. Now," Emily commanded.

Noah quickly worked his way out of them, springing his cock free. She'd seen it before, of course, not to mention felt all of him plunging deep inside her, but she was still amazed how much the sight of it made her mouth water... and how much she craved having him inside her again.

Noah didn't waste any time. He slid her up further on the comforter, lifted one of her legs over his hip, and thrust inside. Her back arched again, and she cried out against the sudden fullness of having all of him.

"You are so tight," he breathed into her neck, his voice hoarse. He slid out and thrust in again. "So hot. My sweet Emily." He thrust again and again, whispering hot words on her skin, holding her tight against the pounding rhythm of his body possessing hers, and making such sweet love that Emily's heart soared with each muttered breath.

She kept bucking against him, meeting him with each thrust. Her pleasure soared so high she was sure the crash back down would shatter her.

She clawed at his back. "Noah," she whispered as she crept closer and closer to the edge. "Oh, God, Noah. Yes!"

"Come for me, my love," he said, his voice hoarse. His pace picked up, and he pounded harder and harder. When her climax finally tipped over the edge, it crashed like an avalanche, burying her in wave after wave of pleasure. She cried out again and again, and dug her fingers into him, holding on for the ride. Eventually, when the waves subsided, she slowed her frantic clawing, but Noah kept moving, slowly, in and out. He was still hard inside her, still pleasuring her by filling her again and again.

"Tell me you really want me," he said, voice strained. He had pulled back to peer into her eyes but was still slowly thrusting in and out, stoking the pleasure engine inside her with a slow, steady thrumming.

Couldn't he tell? "I really want you."

"We can just do this," he said, thrusting a little harder for emphasis. "We can just make love."

She ran her hands over his broad shoulders and up to his gorgeous face. "I want you forever, Noah Wilding."

His eyes closed briefly, then opened. "I have to bite you, Em. Take you from behind and sink my teeth into your sweet, sweet neck. Then my magic will be inside you... forever. You'll be mine. *Forever*. Are you sure?"

She held his cheeks as he made love to her. "This is a dream I didn't even dare to have. Take me, Noah. I'm already yours."

Then he growled that deep, rumbling, possessive sound again, pulled out from her, and commanded, "Turn over."

CHAPTER 17

Emily's sweet body was spread before him.

Noah could hardly believe she wanted this—that she wanted *him*—with all she knew about him and all she'd been through. But he meant every word of his promise. If she would have him, if she would take his bite and his love, he would care for and love her for the rest of his days. He wasn't entirely wolf, and she wasn't wolf at all, but he knew in his heart this was what true mates were—bound by not just magic, but by love.

Even better, he knew what the bond would mean on her side—that she would always feel loved, always cared for, always *safe*. Even if she didn't have magic of her own, he could give her *his* magic, and *that* she would carry with her every minute of every day, enveloping her in a very real manifestation of the love he had for her.

Emily had turned over, just as he asked, and now she was perched on hands and knees on the comforter, waiting for him to take her. Her entire body was flushed with the two orgasms he'd given her so far, and he was dying to bury himself in her again and complete the act... but he had to be sure.

He slid his hand along her tight little bottom and eased up behind her. He nudged her entrance with his cock but didn't push inside.

She peered back at him. "Noah," she said, slightly breathless. "For God's sake, don't tease me."

"It might hurt a little," he warned. He knew the bite might sting. For wolves, they healed quickly, so it wasn't a concern. For a soft, delicious human like Emily, the wound might be more severe.

She reached back to grab his hand, the one cupping her bottom, and then pushed her rear end back on him, nearly drawing his cock inside her. "Then you had better make it feel good first."

God, when she said things like that... the possessive growl of his beast rumbled deep in his chest. He grabbed hold of her hips and thrust inside. She gasped in a way that coursed satisfaction through him. She was so insanely tight—he knew she wasn't used to having him inside, not really, not yet—and it nearly drove him mad with each stroke. The small whimpers coming from her only made him pound harder, ramping up both their pleasure. He slid a hand around to rub her sweet spot, that sensitive nub that was already inflamed from her first two orgasms. He wanted this one to be the best, the ultimate, the one that she would always remember as the beginning of their lives together. For wolves, the mating climax was the best they would ever experience, a magic-charged sexual release that was like nothing else in the world. For him, it would still be that. At least, he thought so. For her, he wasn't so sure.

And the bite... he figured she would feel the bond instantly, as he would, once the magic entered her bloodstream. Maybe that bond would push her climax even higher, even without the normal submission bond that wolves formed before mating. And even without having her own magic in her blood—she would have *his*, and maybe that would be enough.

He could feel his own orgasm building, a coil that ramped tighter with each thrust. He leaned forward over her beautiful body, still thrusting, trying to hold back, trying to keep from coming before her, waiting until they were both ready for this bond that could never be broken. He swept her blonde hair from where it spilled over her shoulder. Her small moans were driving him crazy, along with the quivering of her muscles clenching him. *So close...* his mouth watered, just as it had from the very first time he saw her, and his fangs came out. He bent down to brush them against her tender skin. One hand held her against the pounding—he was still claiming her with his cock, pushing them both higher, right to the peak—and just as her moans turned to shrieks and her body clenched around him, he sank his fangs into her flesh.

She screamed, but it was pleasure taking flight from her body on waves of sound. He clamped his mouth around her, sealing the bite, and allowing his magic to flow into the wound. He pumped her again and again, his cock driving home the mating, and suddenly his release swept over him, drowning him in a tsunami of pleasure that joined him with her, body and soul. As he rode that wave, he could feel his magic draining into her, and suddenly it was as if they were truly one body, one being, writhing in pleasure and awash in magical energy. It permeated every fiber of his being. He wasn't just connected to her through his cock and his bite, but through the invisible threads of magic that would forevermore bind them together.

It lifted him and drained him at the same time. Pleasure and emptying.

He could sense when it was complete, when the magic took hold and cemented.

He released her from his bite with a gasp, then pulled the rest of the way from her and collapsed on the bed. She wobbled, seeming weak from it as well. He pulled her down to him, tucking her against his chest and curling around her small form. He kissed at the puncture wounds, giving them small licks that he hoped might give some measure of faster healing. To his amazement, it worked, and the red spots healed almost instantly.

"Are you all right, my love?" he asked, winded and uplifted. His heart was somewhere in the clouds, and his body was heavy with pleasure on the bed.

"Oh my God." Her voice was as breathless as his.

"Is that a yes?" He almost couldn't laugh, his body too

replete with pleasure and too buzzed out to sustain that kind of motion… but he managed a small huff that shook them both.

"I feel it," she whispered in a voice filled with awe.

"My magic. It's inside you now." He was shocked at how possessive that felt. *His* magic. Forever inside her. She belonged to him, with him, beside him. Always. The wash of pride and joy that swept over him left him unable to say anymore.

She curled and turned in his arms to face him, eyes wide as she peered up at him. "It feels like burning, but it doesn't hurt."

"I'm so glad." He touched her cheek with his fingertips. "I was afraid it might."

She shook her head. "I can feel it. I can feel *you*. It's like…" She pressed her hands flat against his chest. "It's like I have a small piece of your wolf inside me. And it's tied by invisible threads to your… wolf? Your inner witch? I can't tell. But it feels… powerful."

He smiled wide. He loved her smart mind, how she was already in love with the mating bond, analyzing it, examining it, trying to understand it.

"I don't know if I'm a wolf or a witch or a little bit of both." He cupped her cheek. "But Emily Jones, you've just now made me the happiest man on earth."

Her eyes shone at that, and he could feel the pride of it dancing on the magical threads that bound them together. Then her face went solemn. "I feel… like it's growing."

He kissed her softly. "It will take some time for the magic to work through all of your blood. To permeate every cell of your body. The bond will just grow stronger with time. And with repeated matings."

Her eyes went wide. "We get to do that *again?*"

He grinned. "Oh yes. Again and again and again… until you tell me you've had enough."

She smiled. "That might take a while."

"I hope it takes forever." The smile on his face faded as hers grew serious again. "What is it?" he asked, concerned.

She shook her head. "It just feels like… like the wolf part of you that's inside me keeps… *growing.* Like it's filling me up."

He frowned, not sure if that was normal or not. "Does it hurt?"

"No. It feels… amazing." She gave him a tentative smile, and he relaxed.

"I should have asked someone about this," he said, a

small frown marring his joy in this. "I should have figured out what the symptoms were for a human. I shouldn't have—"

She pressed her finger to his lips, stopping him. "You are no ordinary wolf, Noah Wilding. No matter what anyone else said, it would be different for you. For *us.*"

"For us." He grinned. "I like the sound of that."

"You better get used to it." Her smile was impish for a moment before fading again. Then she frowned. "I feel warm. Like that burning is growing stronger... and fuller..." Her eyes unfocused, and suddenly she was pushing away from him on the bed.

"Emily?" His voice hiked up in alarm.

She held her hands up, keeping him back. "I'm okay. I'm—" Then her eyes went wide, and his heart leaped into his throat.

Then, before his very eyes, *she shifted.*

He jolted upright on the bed and stared, mouth hanging open.

Emily had shifted into a white wolf.

"Holy mother of God," he whispered.

Her beautiful blue eyes were wide with surprise... and maybe fear. He couldn't tell, but the bond between them suddenly magnified ten-fold. In a blink, he shifted as well, as if called by her wolf to be in that form together.

Oh my God, Emily! His shocked thoughts sailed over to her.

I'm a wolf. I. Am. A. Wolf! Her gaze flitted all over her new body, down to her paws, back to her tail, along her snowy-white flank. She hopped up on all fours and did a little dance, turning around in place on the bed. Then she stopped and lunged for him, rubbing her muzzle all over his in a sloppy kind of wolfish kiss.

He was still too stunned to react, but it was slowly dawning on him: *she was happy.*

And that was all that mattered to him.

Holy-freaking-awesome, Noah! How did you do this? Her thoughts were scattered and running a million miles an hour, but that much came through coherently.

I don't know, he responded. And that was the flat truth. He had no idea.

Oh my God, I'm reading your THOUGHTS! She was so giddy with this that he couldn't help but feel the joy of it.

He smiled. *That's how it works when you're a wolf.*

She sat back on her haunches again and stared at him, open-mouthed. *It's because you're a witch. Your witch side did this.*

He cocked his head. *That's possible. I honestly have no idea.*

*I just wished…*He held off on sending the rest of that thought.

Wished for what? Her bright blue eyes were intense on him.

That you would experience all of it, all of the bond, he finished. There was no point in keeping anything from her. In fact, he never wanted to keep anything from her ever again.

She nodded her head, then blinked and shook it, probably still not used to the feeling of her wolf form. *You wished this for me… and it came true.* Her eyes were wide again. *And now I can…* She stopped mid-thought and sprung up to her paws again.

He watched as she stretched her front paws forward, raised her rump in the air, tucked her tail and then finally her head.

The submission pose.

The magic of it hit him like a blast of megawatt sunshine. The force of that blast pushed him up into the alpha position, tail erect, ears pointed forward, standing tall on the bed before her.

Rise, my love. The words came automatically to his mind, but it was whirling in utter amazement. Her submission charged him, elated him, and notched into place the completion of the bond between them.

They were fully mated now.

His mouth hung open in surprise again.

Shift for me! he commanded, and in an instant, they were naked together on the bed in their human forms again. Noah grabbed hold of Emily's shoulders. He'd never seen her smile so hard, and his smile was threatening to break his face.

"I can't believe…" Noah fumbled for words. "Do you understand this, Em? We're truly mated now." He gaped at her for a moment, then said, "Please tell me you wanted this."

She gave him a look like he was crazy. "Please tell me I'm not *dreaming* this. Because this is totally a dream. This *has* to be a dream."

He grinned and pulled her down on the bed with him, her small form a gorgeous weight on his chest. "If this is a dream, I don't want to ever wake up."

Then he kissed her again and again. He had no idea how any of it was possible, or how he would explain it to his brother and sister and pack, but he wasn't about to question any of it. He had the woman he loved in his arms, she was fully and completely his mate, and he was making her dreams come true.

He truly couldn't ask for anything more.

CHAPTER 18

Emily felt like a fish in a fishbowl... only she was surrounded by a pack of astonished and disbelieving wolves. Noah had explained that they were mated now—*truly* mated, since she was now a wolf—and it was going over like ticking hand grenade.

His sister, Piper, was the first to speak. "You turned her into a *wolf.*" There couldn't be any more skepticism in her voice. "Using your magical powers as a witch."

She looked to Daniel, their brother, but he was staring

in wide-eyed horror at Noah. Emily was pretty sure he'd already figured out all the implications, including that Daniel and Piper could both be part-witch as well.

"Well, he's certainly got street cred as a witch," Owen said, wryly. He was hanging out at the edge of the great room, next to the front door. Noah had his arm around Emily—he pulled her closer as the silence fell even heavier around them. The three River brothers were gathered along with several others from their pack. Mama River stood by the kitchen door, quietly observing, but not saying anything.

No one was saying anything.

Jaxson spoke up next. "Well, my mate is a half-witch. Maybe the two of you can start a club." He gave Noah a small smile and a nod, and Emily supposed that should be enough—he *was* the alpha of the Riverwise pack where Noah worked, after all.

"That works for me," Jared announced. "Hey, Mama, what's for lunch?" He sauntered toward the kitchen, and that seemed to finally break the tension.

Jace strode forward and clasped hands with Noah. His eyes twinkled as he glanced at Emily. "I can't wait to see this wolf of yours, Ms. Jones. Later, maybe. After the honeymoon." He smirked, shook Noah's hand again, then strode after his older brother, Jared, to the kitchen.

Jaxson was busy ushering people out of the great room as well, saying, "Show's over, folks. Move along."

It was a relief, but Piper was still staring at her like she was some kind of creature that crawled out of the black lagoon, and Daniel was staring off into space. Owen stayed by the door, silent, watching and apparently waiting for Daniel to come out of his fugue.

"Maybe I should…?" Emily gestured up the stairs. She was more than willing to leave them alone to discuss their family matters.

"No," Noah said softly. "You're my family now."

That made her glow from the very center of her being. She stayed tucked under his arm.

Daniel still looked dazed. "What does this mean?" he asked. Emily wasn't sure who it was directed at, but she wasn't about to offer up an explanation.

"I don't understand all of it," Noah said quietly, so their voices wouldn't carry over the noise of the still-retreating shifter crowd. "All I know is that Dad was an asshole, so it's not hard to guess that his bio-dad was as well. But we make our own paths, man. I'm not going to be like either one of them."

"Well, of course, you're not," Piper said, irritation

plain on her face. "You're my kid brother, which means you clearly have awesome stamped in your DNA." She waved vaguely at Noah's body. "Whatever that DNA is these days."

"Thanks a lot." But Noah was grinning again, and that washed relief through Emily.

"So, at any moment, I could turn into a witch." Daniel's hundred-yard stare had finally come back to the safehouse… and it was drilling into his brother.

Noah rubbed the back of his neck. "Look, I don't know. You were only in the cages for what, a day? Did they inject anything important into you? Any serums?" Emily knew Daniel had been captured briefly in his attempts to rescue Cassie, one of his cousins in the sprawling Wilding family packs. Cassie was just a kid, younger sister of Terra Wilding, the Seattle artist.

Daniel frowned. "I wouldn't know. I was unconscious most of the time. But it was short—a few hours at most." He looked visibly freaked out.

"Then you're probably fine." Noah shrugged. "Whatever happens, however it turns out, it doesn't matter. We're still family. We're still pack. We're in this together."

Daniel blinked and stared at the floor for a few

moments. When he finally looked up, he looked straight into Noah's eyes. "I've been a pretty shitty brother, haven't I?"

Emily could see the emotion flash across Noah's face. "No. No way. You've always been there when I needed you."

Daniel reached out, and Emily ducked out just in time not to get caught in the manly hug between them. She had to blink back her tears, but Piper was letting them just drop down her face.

She turned to Emily. "Hormones. I'm allowed to cry." Then she joined Daniel and Noah, hugging both her brothers at once.

Emily grinned but stepped back and let them have their space. And wiped at the tears threatening the corners of her eyes.

Owen was nodding and grinning by the door. "Hey," he said softly to her. "Welcome to the wolfing world." He looked amused with himself. "I've never had occasion to say that before."

"I'm still getting used to it myself." But she smiled wide at him.

Was she really part of this world now? This loose association of shifters and family and friends and pack?

She would feel lost, except… in the strangest of ways, it felt like coming home. Her own family had never been there for her, not when she really needed it. She'd always been a *lone wolf* in a human sort of way. And now, all of sudden, she was mated and accepted in a world she had only fantasized about.

Definitely the best day of her life.

Daniel, Piper, and Noah finally broke apart their hug with teary faces, mostly on Piper, and embarrassed looks, mostly on Daniel.

"So, what's our status with this damn threat against WildLove?" Noah asked. He was directing it at Owen as well. Emily figured he and Daniel must have been working with the rest of Riverwise to straighten out the mess they'd left behind—with the WildLove office blown up and nothing but ash left of their best lead on the hate group.

"Well, we've still got that first bomber locked up in a cottage out back," Owen said. "With the second bomber turned to ash, and WildLove down for the count, at least for the moment, I'd say we lie low for a while. See what happens."

"I made a backup, you know," Emily piped up.

They all turned to her. She shrugged. "I'm a

ALISA WOODS

programmer, what do you expect? We could get back online pretty quickly with WildLove if we need to hunt down more bad guys."

Noah grinned. "Why does it not surprise me that you're not scared off by any of this?"

She tucked her hand around his muscular arm. "I just don't want any more shifters to get hurt."

"She's right," Daniel said. "We still don't know if these guys were working with the Wolf Hunter or not. They could have just been vigilantes. Independents."

Emily frowned. "Maybe this guy, the one who's ash now, actually *was* the Wolf Hunter."

Noah pulled her closer. "Why do you think that?"

"Well, he had a mask," she said. "And he *was* making a video of his plan to, well, kill me."

"You don't have to talk about this, Em." Noah's face was a picture of concern.

"It's fine," she said, waving it away. "My point is that he sure acted like he was part of something bigger. Like he had major plans for that database of shifters he wanted from WildLove."

"So, maybe you just killed our bad guy?" Piper asked Noah.

"That sure would be nice," Owen said. "Won't know

until all this madness blows over, though."

"So we lay low," Noah said. "Just like you suggested."

"I'll work with Marjorie on resurrecting WildLove," Emily said. "If I know her, she's already spooling up investors to renovate the building. But we won't go live until we're sure the threat is contained."

Noah gave her a nod and a squeeze. "In the meantime, maybe we can work on that honeymoon."

"Honeymoon?" she asked, giving him the side-eye. "Don't you need to be married to have one of those?"

His eyes glittered. "I thought you would never ask."

Her mouth dropped open. Then Noah smirked and dropped to one knee. "Emily Jones, I don't have a ring, but if you don't marry me, I'm probably going to break down and cry in front of all my family. And Owen."

Her mouth wasn't working. It just flopped open and closed like a dying fish. Finally, she managed, "You're kidding."

"Not even a little bit." Noah smiled up at her, waiting.

Piper leaned in close to her. "It's part of that *forever* mating thing, honey. Just go with it."

"I... um... yes?" Emily said, still flustered.

"Yes?" Noah asked, eyebrow raised.

"Yes," she said, more definitively. "I will definitely

marry you. Sometime. In the future. When I get over my shock and have my mouth functioning again."

Noah popped up from the floor. "Deal! Now, let's see if that mouth works." Then he kissed her in front of all of them, and she completely forgot to be flustered. Owen clapped his hands, applauding them behind her, and she was pretty sure Piper and Daniel were ribbing their brother in some way, but she didn't care about any of that. All she knew was that her magical dream had just gotten even better.

A knock at the door interrupted their make-out fest in the great room, just as everyone was starting to wander away.

"No, please, continue!" Owen said sarcastically to them, waving his hands with effusive encouragement. "Allow me to get it."

He opened the door. Outside stood a large man in a uniform. A *police* uniform.

All the hairs on Emily's arms rose at once.

"Is there a Terra Wilding on the premises?" the officer asked. Emily peered at his Seattle Police Department badge and the embroidered name on his shirt pocket. *Officer Grant.* He was tall and broad, taking up most of the door frame, and his eyes were chiseled blue. His short, dark hair was almost the same color of midnight black as his uniform.

Noah stepped forward. "What's this about, officer?"

"I was told Terra Wilding was residing here at the moment?" Officer Grant's expression was stone cold.

"Told by *whom?*" Daniel asked, stepping up to join Owen and Noah at the door. The tension rocketed through the roof. It was the three shifter men against one human police officer, and if it were Emily on the receiving end of those hostile stares, she'd be quaking in her sneakers.

Officer Grant seemed unfazed. "By the recent video released this morning. By someone who calls himself the Wolf Hunter—ring any bells?" He calmly looked each one of them in the eye. "This address was listed as her current residence. Given the bombing at the WildLove building downtown, this matter has been bumped in priority."

"Bumped in priority?" Noah scowled at him, and Emily could guess what was going through his mind. The police were no friends of shifters. Up until now, there had been all kinds of death threats against wolves, experiments conducted by the government, hate videos and demonstrations… and the police had pretty much looked the other way. All along, shifters were considered part of the criminal underground, not regular citizens that should be protected. More often than not, going into police custody just ended up with shifters being fingerprinted for future identification in the crimes they might commit.

Officer Grant's rock-hard expression gave no impression that any of that had changed. "Yes, sir, the bombing must have pissed off someone important. Because you shifter lot just got bumped up to our number one priority." He paused. "And I've been assigned to Terra Wilding's case."

Want more Wilding Pack?
WILD HEAT (Wilding Pack Wolves 3)

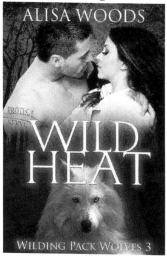

He's a hot cop.
She's a wild artist.
Making art was never so dangerously SEXY.
Get WILD HEAT today!

Subscribe to Alisa's newsletter to know when a new book
is coming out!
http://smarturl.it/AlphaLoversNews

ABOUT THE AUTHOR

Alisa Woods lives in the Midwest with her husband and family, but her heart will always belong to the beaches and mountains where she grew up. She writes sexy paranormal romances about alpha men and the women who love them. She enjoys exploring the struggles we all have, where we resist—and succumb to—our most tempting vices as well as our greatest desires. She firmly believes that love triumphs over all.

All of Alisa's romances feature sexy alphas and the strong women who love them.

23825062R00157

Printed in Poland
by Amazon Fulfillment
Poland Sp. z o.o., Wrocław